JUDGES' CITATION

With enormous power and wonderful subtlety, Meron Hadero grants us access to the inner worlds of people at moments when everything is at risk. In the stories that make up *A Down Home Meal for These Difficult Times*, the emotional stakes are high. In "The Suitcase," on her first-ever visit with family in the city of her birth, a young woman finds herself paralyzed by the pressure of bridging the distance between relatives who left and those who stayed. In "Kind Stranger," a woman on a brief return visit to Addis Ababa—Hadero's characters are usually out of place, struggling to move backward or forward to a place that resembles home—is waylaid on the street by a man with a terrible burden to relieve.

Often the material stakes are breathtakingly high, too: A street sweeper who pins his hopes on a smooth-talking NGO employee; the residents of a village who, displaced by drought, fill their pockets with seeds and set out on foot for somewhere with water.

That closeness to the edge—of safety, of the known and being known—will resonate with all of us whose lives have been marked by border crossings, whether by choice or, more likely, because of complex political and environmental forces far beyond our control. As we enter a future that will be shaped more and more profoundly by such border crossings, these sharp, humane, beautiful portraits are a gift.

—PRIZE JUDGES DINAW MENGESTU, ACHY OBEJAS,
AND ILAN STAVANS

A DOWN HOME MEAL FOR THESE DIFFICULT TIMES

Stories

MERON HADERO

RESTLESS BOOKS
Brooklyn, New York

First Restless Books hardcover edition June 2022

This book is supported in part by an award from the National Endowment for the Arts.
This book is made possible by the New York State Council on the Arts with the support of Governor Kathy Hochul and the New York State Legislature.

Hardcover ISBN: 9781632061188
Library of Congress Control Number: 2021948385

Cover design by Emily Comfort
Text design by Sarah Schneider

Printed in the United States of America

1 3 5 7 9 10 8 6 4 2

Restless Books, Inc.
232 3rd Street, Suite A101
Brooklyn, NY 11215

www.restlessbooks.org
publisher@restlessbooks.org

For my parents

Contents

*He who has a hundred miles to walk should
reckon ninety as half the journey*

—*Zen in the Art of Archery,*
quoting a proverb

A DOWN HOME MEAL

FOR THESE DIFFICULT TIMES

The Suitcase

On Saba's last day in Addis Ababa, she had just one unchecked to-do left on her long and varied list, which was to explore the neighborhood on her own, even though she'd promised her relatives that she would always take someone with her when she left the house. But she was twenty, a grown-up, and wanted to know that on her first-ever trip to this city of her birth, she'd gained at least some degree of independence and assimilation. So it happened that Saba had no one to turn to when she got to the intersection around Meskel Square and realized she had seen only one functioning traffic light in all of Addis Ababa, population four million by official counts, though no one here seemed to trust official counts, and everyone assumed it was much more crowded, certainly too crowded for just one traffic light. That single, solitary, lonely little traffic light in this mushrooming metropolis was near the old National Theater, not too far from the UN offices, the presidential palace, the former African Union—a known, respected part of the city located an unfortunate mile (a disobliging 1.6 kilometers) away from where Saba stood before a sea of cars contemplating a difficult crossing.

Small nimble vehicles, Fiats and VW Bugs, skimmed the periphery of the traffic, then seemed to be flung off centrifugally, almost gleefully, in some random direction. The center was a tangled cluster of cars slowly crawling along paths that might take an automobile backward, forward, sideward. In the middle of this jam was a sometimes visible traffic cop whose tense job seemed to be avoiding getting hit while keeping one hand slightly in the air. He was battered by curses, car horns, diesel exhaust, as he nervously shielded his body and tried to avoid these assaults. Saba quickly saw she couldn't rely on him to help her get across. She dipped her foot from the curb onto the street, and a car raced by, so she retreated. A man walked up next to her and said in English, "True story, I know a guy who crossed the street halfway and gave up."

Saba looked at the stranger. "Pardon, what was that?"

"He had been abroad for many years and came back expecting too much," the man said, now speaking as slowly as Saba. "That sad man lives on the median at the ring road. I bring him books sometimes," he said slyly, taking one out of his messenger bag and holding it up. "A little local wisdom. Don't start what you can't finish." Saba watched the stranger dangle his toes off the curb, lean forward, backward, forward and back and then, as if becoming one with the flow of the city, lunge into the traffic and disappear from her sight until he reemerged on the opposite sidewalk. "Miraculous," Saba said to herself as he turned, pointed at her, then held up the book again. Saba tried to follow his lead and set her body to the rhythm of the cars, swaying forward and back, but couldn't find the beat.

As she was running through her options, a line of idling taxis became suddenly visible when a city bus turned the corner. She realized that as impractical as it seemed, she could hail a cab to get her across the busy street. The trip took ten minutes; the fare cost fifteen USD, for she was unable to negotiate a better rate, though at least she'd found a way to the other side. She turned back to see the taxi driver leaning out the window talking to a few people, gesturing at her, laughing, and she knew just how badly she'd fumbled yet another attempt to fit in. All month Saba had failed almost every test she'd faced, and though she'd seized one last chance to see if this trip had changed her, had taught her at least a little of how to live in this culture, she'd only ended up proving her relatives right: she wasn't even equipped to go for a walk on her own. What she thought would be a romantic, monumental reunion with her home country had turned out to be a fiasco; she didn't belong here.

She was late getting back to her uncle Fassil's house, where family and friends of family were waiting for her to say goodbye, to chat and eat and see her one last time, departures being even more momentous than arrivals. Twelve chairs had been moved into the cramped living room. Along with the three couches, they transformed the space into a theater packed with guests, each of whom sat with his or her elbows pulled in toward the torso to make space for all. They came, they said, to offer help, but she sensed it was the kind of help that gave—and took.

It was time to go, and she was relieved when Fassil said—in English for her benefit—"We are running out of time, so we have already started to fill this one for you." He pointed past the suitcase that Saba packed before her walk and gestured to a second, stuffed with items and emitting the faint scent of a kitchen after mealtime. At her mother's insistence, Saba had brought one suitcase for her own clothes and personal items and a second that, for the trip there, was full of gifts from America—new and used clothes, old books, magazines, medicine—to give to family she had never met. For her return, it would be full of gifts to bring to America from those same relatives and family friends.

Saba knew this suitcase wasn't just a suitcase. She'd heard there was no DHL here, no UPS. Someone thought there was FedEx, but that was just for extremely wealthy businessmen. People didn't trust the government post. So Saba's suitcase offered coveted real estate on a vessel traveling between here and there. Everyone wanted a piece; everyone fought to stake a claim to their own space. If they couldn't secure a little spot in some luggage belonging to a traveling friend, they'd send nothing at all. The only reasonable alternative would be to have the items sent as freight on a cargo ship, and how reasonable was that? The shipping container would sail from Djibouti on the Red Sea (and with all the talk of Somali pirates, this seemed almost as risky as hurling a box into the ocean and waiting for the fickle tides). After the Red Sea, a cargo ship that made it through the Gulf of Aden would go south on the Indian Ocean, around the Cape of Good Hope, across the Atlantic, through the Panama Canal, to the Pacific, up the American coast to Seattle. An empty suitcase opened up a rare direct link between two worlds, so Saba understood why relatives and friends wanted to fill her bag with carefully wrapped food things, gifts, sundry items, making space, taking space, moving and shifting the bulging contents of the bag.

Fassil placed a scale in front of Saba and set to zeroing it. She leaned over the scale as he nudged the dial to the right. The red needle moved ever so slightly, so incredibly slightly that Saba doubted it worked at all, but then Fassil's hand slipped, the needle flew too far, to the other side of zero. He pushed the dial just a hair to the left now, and the red needle swung back by a full millimeter. He nudged the dial again; now it stuck.

"Fassil, Saba has to go," Lula said, shaking her hands like she was flicking them dry. "Let's get going. Her flight leaves in three hours, and with the traffic from all the construction around Meskel Square and Bole Road . . . ."

Saba leaned toward that wobbly needle as Fassil used his fingernail to gently coax the dial a breath closer. A tap, nearly there. A gentle pull.

"Looks good, Fassil," Saba said kindly but impatiently.

"It has to be precise," Fassil replied, then turned to the gathered crowd. "Look what you're making the poor girl carry." He pointed to that second suitcase.

Saba tried to lift it, but it was as heavy as an ox. Fassil rushed over and helped her pick it up, and when he felt its weight, he said, "There's no way they'll let her take this." The room hummed with disapproval, punctuated with tsks and clicked tongues. "I can just pay the fee," Saba quickly said, but Lula stood again, put up her hands and boomed, "You will not pay a fee. It's too much money. You are our guest, and our guest will pay no fee!"

"It's okay," Saba said. "If we must, we must." But now the resistance came from everyone. Saba looked helplessly at Fassil. "Let me pay. I have to go. What else can I do?" she asked. She looked at the others and wondered if this was one of those times when a "no" was supposed to be followed by a "Please, yes!" "No, no." "Really, I insist." "No, we couldn't," "Really, yes you must." "Okay." "Okay." Was it that kind of conversation? That call and response? Or was it the other kind, the "No, no!" "Really, I insist!" "No, we just couldn't." "Okay, no then."

"Of course you can't pay. They will never let you," Fassil said, ending Saba's deliberation. He announced, "I'll weigh the suitcase," and there was a general sigh of approval. "But," Fassil continued, "if it's overweight, which it is, we are going to have to make some tough choices." He turned to Saba. "You are going to have to make some tough choices." She nodded and hoped silently that it would come in at weight, please. If she could be granted one earthly wish in this moment, that was what she would wish for. She watched Fassil heave the suitcase onto the scale and winced as the needle that hovered, almost vibrated, above zero shot to the right. Thirty kilos—ten kilos too heavy.

The crowd began to murmur anxiously, and a few shouted out sounds of frustration. Then one by one, the guests began to speak in turn, as if pleading their cases before a judge. Konjit was the first up. She was old, at least eighty, a verified elder who settled disputes and brokered weddings and divorces, part of that council of respected persons that otherwise held a neighborhood together. As Konjit walked toward Saba, Saba bowed a little.

"Norr," Saba said, a sign of respect.

"Bugzer," Konjit replied, acknowledging that the order of things hadn't been completely turned on its head. Konjit lifted the edge of her shawl, flung it around her shoulder and walked slowly right up to the suitcase and unzipped it. She took out a package of chickpeas and tossed them on the ground, and though someone grumbled at this, Konjit just smoothed her pressed hair behind her ears as if she were calming herself before an important announcement, an orator about to make a speech, an actress set to perform. Konjit held a hand up and waited for total silence. Then she turned to Saba, put her hands on both her hips, which swayed as she stepped closer, and said in a low voice that filled the small space, "Please, Sabayaye, I haven't seen my grandchildren since they were two years old. How old are you?"

"Twenty," Saba said apologetically.

"Twenty? Ah, in all the time you've been alive in this world I have not seen them. Imagine! I'm old now. Who can even say how old I am? I'm too old to count and getting older. I want to send this bread so they know people here love them."

Most of the others in the room nodded in agreement, but not Rahel. Rahel shook her head as she stood from the couch and walked right up to Konjit, putting a hand on Konjit's arm. "Who can say how old you are, Konjit? Me, I can say how old you are. Not the number of years, of course, but I can say for sure that I am older than you. One month, remember."

Rahel brought up that one-month position of seniority often, and Saba had come to expect it. Within just her first week there, Saba learned that Rahel and Konjit had grown up and grown old fighting often about things like which church had the most blessed holy water, Ledeta (Rahel) or Giorgis (Konjit), or whether it was better to use white teff flour (Konjit) or brown teff flour (Rahel), or where you could get the best deals on textiles, Mercato (Konjit) or Sheromeda (Rahel). Without fail, each argument ended with Rahel staking out a win by virtue of being slightly elder.

Rahel bent down and removed one of the three loaves of bread from the suitcase and tried to hand it back to Konjit, who refused to take it. Saba, wanting to hurry things along, reached out for the loaf, but Rahel placed the bread on the floor by her feet. "You can bake a loaf, Konjit, I give you that, but it takes you three hours to make that bread? Eh? I spent two days—two days—making this beautiful doro wat for my nephew. The power kept switching off. I had to go to Bole to freeze it in Sintayu's freezer, and she has all those kids and all those in-laws and hardly any space in her house, let alone her freezer, but still, that's what it took to make this beautiful wat. Then, I had to wrap the container so tight that, should any melt in transit, it will stay safe and secure—and with these old, old, old fingers," she said, putting up her index, middle and ring finger. "Can you believe it? These old, old fingers," she said, now

7

raising her pinky and thumb. "These fingers a month older than yours, Konjit." She pulled Saba over and put her fanned fingers on Saba's left shoulder, leaning on her. "Just take this beautiful wat for me. It will be no problem, right?"

Before Saba could say that this seemed reasonable, Wurro walked up to Saba, and Saba shifted her attention again. "I may not be the oldest, and my hands don't ache like Rahel's, but please, think about this objectively, Saba," said Wurro, whose utilitarian views led her to make obviously questionable decisions like employing fifteen workers in her small grocery so that fifteen more paychecks went out each month and fifteen more families would be happy, even if it put her one family on the verge of ruin. Wurro never argued her utilitarian views as forcefully, though, as when they matched her own purposes. She cleared her throat, and Saba waited for what she feared would be another well-argued plea. Wurro began, "If you don't send this bread, Konjit, your family will still eat bread. If you don't send this wat, Rahel, your family will still eat wat." Wurro took Saba's hand, and said, "My niece had a difficult pregnancy. You have to take this gunfo because if you don't take it, well, there is no way to get gunfo in America, and who has ever heard of a woman not eating gunfo after labor? If you don't bring it, she won't have it. Milk for the baby, gunfo for the mother. It's natural logic. You can't deny it."

"But American women don't eat gunfo. Do they eat gunfo, Saba?" asked Lula.

"She's never been pregnant in America, right? How would she know?" asked Wurro.

"She's never been pregnant here. Does she even know gunfo?" Konjit asked.

Saba said, "I know gunfo," and was met with whispered words of approval, so she refrained from adding how hard she had to swallow to get a spoonful down of the thick paste made from corn, wheat, barley, or banana root, she wasn't even sure. Whatever gunfo was, she'd rather not bring it if it were up to her, but she wasn't actually sure of that, either. Was it up to her?

"Saba is a smart girl," Lula said. "She probably read at least ten books in the four weeks she was here." Saba felt guilty then, because it was true that she had declined as many invitations as she accepted, choosing sometimes to read alone at home. "She must know Americans have high-tech things for women after their pregnancies. They don't need gunfo," Lula said, rearranging the contents of the suitcase to make room for her own package. "But you know what they do need in America? Have you ever tasted American butter?"

Lula looked at the others as if this would end the discussion. She stood up, opened her arms. "Have you had American butter?" No one spoke. Saba kept quiet, for of course she had eaten American butter, but what good would it do to mention that now? Besides, few had the courage to challenge strong-willed Lula, even with the truth.

"No one here has ever had American butter, so then that settles it." Lula took out another of Konjit's loaves of bread and a bag of roasted grains. "I have eaten American butter. I have tasted it with my own tongue. I can say with certainty that American butter is only the milk part, no spices, no flavor. It just tastes like fat. Please bring this butter to my best friend for her wedding banquet," Lula said with her hands now pressed over her heart and looking pleadingly at Saba. "Ahwe, her wedding! And what a feat to get that man to the altar. His gambling and staying out late and—"

"Whee, whee," Konjit interrupted, shaking her head and removing Lula's butter and putting a second loaf back into the suitcase. "You want her to bring butter so your friend can marry a bad man? Have you ever heard such nonsense?" Konjit asked Saba. Saba shrugged, and Konjit said, "See, she has never heard such nonsense," and Saba didn't have the heart to correct her and didn't have the heart not to correct her, and she didn't know which would have helped her bring this to the right resolution, so she just made a vague gesture and let them finish.

"He is not a bad man, just a *man* man," Lula said.

"Well, my son is a good man raising good grandchildren. Lula, my son brought you the stretchy pants you asked for from America when he visited. Wurro, my son brought you a laptop last time he came. Rahel, he brought you cereal with raisins, the kind you always ask for. Fassil, he brought you books, since you have long gone through everything at every library here, I assume. Saba, one day if you stay longer in Ethiopia, he will bring you something, too, anything you ask. Name something you miss here."

"Too much talk, Konjit!" Rahel yelled. "The traffic, she has to go!"

Konjit swatted away Rahel's interruption and gestured to Saba. Saba tried to think of what to say. She didn't want to offend them by making them believe she had lacked for anything. She remembered how hurt Konjit had been when Saba visited after lunchtime, only to find a full meal waiting for her. When Saba declined it, Konjit insisted that the dishes were very clean and the food fresh. That wasn't as bad, though, as sitting down to eat "just a little," and passing on the salad, the water, the cheese, the fruit, eating only the lentils and bread, accepting some coffee but not even the milk. "You have all been so kind to me," Saba said, bowing respectfully, pronouncing all her syllables perfectly, precisely as quickly as she could. "I have not missed a thing. But it's late, and it's true, the traffic is bad . . . ."

Konjit dismissed Saba. "She has learned the Ethiopian way. Good girl. Too polite to say you need anything here." Konjit put an arm on Saba's shoulder and continued, "Okay, don't tell us, that's okay. But if you visit again to stay awhile, and if you find you are homesick for something you grew accustomed to there in America, my son will bring it. He is a good son. I am asking you to take two loaves of bread. Okay, forget about the third, I don't want to ask too much of you, even though I am an old lady who has not seen her grandchildren in, oh, who knows how long. But these two loaves must stay in the suitcase, two loaves for my three grandchildren so they know I am thinking about them. That I have not forgotten them." Saba could see that Konjit was too proud to say what she really meant: she didn't want her grandchildren to forget about her, a fear she must bear, living so far away for so many years with only limited lines of connection.

Konjit's argument hung there in the air until Fikru stood hesitantly and walked over to the suitcase, finding his bags of spices on the floor beside it. He reached into the suitcase and took out three Amharic-English dictionaries and tossed them on the coffee table. Hanna shouted out, "Aye! Why, Fikru, would you do that?" She ran over and picked up the books, then threw them back in, but Konjit took them out, for they crushed her bread.

Fikru, who kept opening his mouth to speak, but found himself overpowered by the more forceful voices, seized his opportunity like a fourth-chair orchestral musician stealing a flourish at the end of a number. He stood next to an overwhelmed Saba and said, "Everyone here has a relative in Seattle, yes? Then why is it that only my son is going to pick Saba up from the airport?" He turned to the others. "You talk about what so-and-so needs or has done, but my son, without asking for anything, has volunteered to get her. He will be carrying this heavy suitcase to his car. Then he will take her to her dorm and bring this heavy suitcase up the stairs if there are stairs or down the hall, should there be a hall. What can it hurt to bring a few items for him?" Fikru showed Saba his items. "Just a few bags of spices: corrorima, grain of paradise, berbere. Please, Saba, a humble parcel for my humble son."

Saba turned to her uncle, Fassil, and discreetly pointed to her watch. "Okay, you all have something to say," Fassil offered, cutting off the remaining guests who gathered around the suitcase, eager to make their appeals. "But the traffic!"

"Yes, the traffic," said Fikru. "The traffic," Rahel and Konjit said in unison, and Lula nodded. Fassil turned to Saba. She asked him, "What do you want to do?" "What do you want to do?" Fassil asked her. Though each person in that room had his or her body turned to the suitcase, all eyes were on Saba, who was trying to figure out how to navigate this scene. They looked her over and imagined she looked so . . . what? Different? Just . . . apart with her woven bag, which intermittently glowed with the light from her iPhone or beeped and pinged and vibrated from the sound of her other gadgetry, her American jeans tucked into tall leather boots, a white button-down shirt and gold earrings, while they wore modest clothes and hand-me-downs, some of which she had brought herself.

She had been in the country one whole month and had tried, they must know, to learn the culture, to reacquaint herself with her first home and fit in. And now, here she stood, on the last moments of her last day, still not sure what to do, while they looked at her lovingly and with curiosity, too. Saba felt the weight of choosing what should be taken and what should be left behind. She was looking for a way out and a way in, but she realized there really were no shortcuts here.

"You have all been so kind," Saba said. "Rahel, you took me to listen to the Azmaris sing," she said, omitting that she had been too shy to dance such unfamiliar dances no matter how encouraging Rahel had been. A few days later, Rahel came back to take her to one of the fancy new hotels where an American cover band played to a foreign crowd, and Saba pretended to like being there. She imagined Rahel had pretended, too.

"Wurro, you took me to the holiday dinner, and we ate that delicious raw meat," Saba said, of course not mentioning that Fassil had to take her to the clinic the next day to get Cipro for her stomach cramps.

"Fikru, you brought me to Mercato to buy a dress," Saba said. But what she most remembered was spending the trip chasing after him through the labyrinthine alleyways; every so often, when Fikru looked back at her, she would wave, and smile, and he'd keep going, losing her twice.

She remembered the man with the messenger bag that morning, the one who had crossed the street, and his warning about starting things you can't finish or giving up too soon. Saba walked to the suitcase she had packed herself, filled with her own things, and in one quick gesture opened it, emptied the contents. Her best clothes fell to the floor: her favorite old jeans, most sophisticated dresses, her one polished blazer, a new pair of rain boots, T-shirts collected from concerts and trips and old relationships. She pushed this empty suitcase to the center of the room.

"Dear friends, neighbors and relatives," she said in forced Amharic, looking at the confused expressions that confronted her, "please, now there is room for it all."

There were gasps, whispers, whistles, an inexplicable loud thud, but no laughter.

"Are you sure?" Fikru asked.

"This is the least I can do," Saba said slowly. "It is the least I can do."

"What about your belongings?" Fassil asked.

"We'll keep them safe for her in case she returns," Konjit said, her voice commanding the space. "Until she returns," Rahel corrected. "Until you return?" Konjit asked, and Saba said yes. Fassil got a bag, put Saba's things in, and told her he would store it in his own closet. With no time to spare, the two suitcases were packed, weighed (the room applauded when both came in just under the limit), and thrown into the trunk of Fassil's car, which sagged a little in the rear. There were three cars in their little caravan that headed to the airport. The ride was slow. The weight of the over-full cars possibly complicated the trip, as did the rocky side streets and, of course, the congestion at the difficult intersections. They pressed on, and they reached the airport in time for Saba to say quick, heartfelt goodbyes and thank-yous, make fresh promises, then pull the two big suitcases onto a luggage cart. Her family and friends of family watched from the waiting area as she hurried to the line to get her boarding pass. They looked on as the two suitcases were weighed and thrown on the screening belt, and they saw her pass the main checkpoint. Every time she looked back to the lobby, she could catch glimpses of them on tiptoe, waiting to see if they might connect with her one more time.

The Wall

When I met Herr Weill, I was a lanky ten-year-old, a fish out of water in —, Iowa, a small college town surrounded by fields in every direction. My family had moved to the US a few weeks earlier from Ethiopia via Berlin, so I knew no English, but was fluent in Amharic and German. I'd speak those sometimes to strangers or just mumble under my breath to say what was on my mind, never getting an answer until the day I met Herr Weill.

I was wearing jeans with a button-down, a too-big blazer, and a clip-on tie waiting in line during what I'd later come to know as a typical mid-'80s Midwest community potluck, with potato salad, pasta salad, green bean casserole, bean salad casserole, tuna pasta salad casserole, a good three-quarters of the dishes on offer incorporating crushed potato chips and dollops of mayonnaise. The Norman Borlaug Community Center had welcomed us because one of the local bigwigs was in the Peace Corps in his student days, and he'd cultivated an interest in global humanitarianism. He'd heard of the new stream of refugees leaving communist dictatorships in

the Third World, found us through the charity that gave us housing in Berlin, and had arranged for the NBCC to orient us, get us
some new used clothes and a place to live. They also invited us to
Sunday meals that were the best ones of my week.

On this particular Sunday, I'd walked into the recreational
room transformed by paper cutouts of pumpkins and bundled
ears of multicolored corn. Cotton had been pulled thin across the
windows, and dried leaves pressed in wax paper taped to the wall.
Beneath a banner (which I couldn't read) was a plastic poster of a
woman with a pointed black hat on her head, her legs straddling
a broom, haunting grimace bearing missing teeth, as if I didn't
already feel afraid and alienated in that space. Next to this mon-
strosity stood a very benign-looking real-life man with a wool scarf
and wool coat, who wiped away a bead of sweat as he eyed, then
looked away from, then eyed again a pretty woman across the room
who was picking through a basket of miniature candy bars.

In German I said to no one in particular, "Why doesn't he just
talk to her?" Nodding at the man with the wool coat, I continued,
"What's he waiting for, permission from his mother?"

Then from a deep voice behind me, I heard in German, "There
was a woman in my life, once. I looked at her the same way."

When this stranger spoke these words, I recalled the moment
a few months back in West Berlin when I was playing soccer with
Herman and Ismail, two Turkish brothers who lived on Friedrich-
strasse next door to me. Our improvised playground was this plot
close to the Berlin Wall where someone had tied a piece of yarn
between two old halogen lamps, a makeshift goal post. Sometimes
I'd aim not for those feet between the metal posts, but far beyond
the wall. This was in defiance of my mother's strict command to
stay away from "that horror of a serpent." Wasteful and risky, she
called it when I'd told her twice before that I'd sacrificed a soccer

ball to the GDR. She was wrong to worry that I'd get in trouble for my antics—I never did. But she was right that I'd been wasteful. We had nothing as it was, and the embarrassment of buying a toy must have been infuriating to her because strangers slandered her with cries of "welfare woman" and "refugee scum" when she walked down the street anyway, just to get groceries or some exercise, and when they saw her carrying something as frivolous as a soccer ball, they'd shout louder, with more spit in their breaths and more rage in their eyes. I knew this, I'd even witnessed this, but for some reason I couldn't help that sometimes, after running circles in the tiny paved playground that pressed against the barricade, I'd visualized this little grounded balloon between my feet soaring to the other side of that imposing wall that seemed to challenge my very sense of freedom, and so I'd close my eyes and kick hard. Herman and Ismail could never—or would never—clear the hurdle, but I'd done it twice already, and the third time I launched the ball just over the barbed wire, I heard a loud grunt from somewhere beyond, and saw the ball come soaring back toward us. I caught it and was stunned. Herman and Ismail yelled at me to send it over again, but I knew it would have broken my heart some if we'd kicked it back and never had it returned. I'd have held tight to hope, I'd have gone back to that spot and waited, I'd have lingered in the playground anticipating a reply, whether or not another ever came. So I convinced Herman and Ismail that we should retire our game, and to make sure of it, I put a pin through the ball and let out the air.

This is how I felt standing in the potluck line that October day looking at the man looking at a woman, hearing this response in German said back to me, the first words I'd understood in this new country spoken by anyone other than my parents: "There was a woman in my life, once. I looked at her the same way," the man had said in German, and I replayed this in my mind as I stood there frozen, not daring to say a thing, holding on to my words like I held that returned ball in the playground.

Johannes Weill went ahead and introduced himself and said everyone just called him Herr Professor Weill or simply Herr Weill because he once was a dean at the college who'd won some big international award, and so it stuck. He told me I was famous in town, too. I pointed at myself, wondering what he'd heard. "You're one of the Ethiopian refugees, right?" Herr Weill asked, then said, "I've been waiting to meet you, the whole town has been talking." I nodded, just beginning to trust in this conversation, in the sincere interest of his tone, in his perfect German, in which he continued, "To answer your question, the man in the wool coat is trying to think of a way to impress the girl, of course."

"Stringing together a sentence might be a good start," I suggested. "His opener is obvious. As she's picking through the basket of candy, ask her what kind of chocolate she likes."

Herr Weill took off his round glasses and squinted in a way that severely exaggerated the already deep lines that crossed his face. He held his glasses up to the light, like he had to make sure that I was real and not a speck on his lens or something, and after this pause, he replied, "It's not always easy to find the right words, you know."

"Maybe you just have to know the right language," I said.

"Well if you don't learn English soon, you'll end up like that man in the wool coat, with no way to say what's on your mind or in your heart, except to some old German guy you met waiting for spaghetti and ham-balls," he said. "And that doesn't sound like a good way to spend a childhood."

"Yeah, I'm working on it," I said.

"I could teach you English."

"Then you must not know," I said. The part I didn't say was "just how poor we are."

By now I was taking modest spoonfuls from the big Tupperware containers so as not to show just how poor we were. Not to overstate how eager I was for spaghetti and ham-balls, I pursed my lips to hide my watering mouth, and turned away hoping he wouldn't hear the faint rumbling of my stomach.

"It's true," Herr Weill said. "I didn't teach languages. I was a professor in the arts, but I do know how to teach."

"But a tutor costs money, and the problem is—"

"A money issue?" he asked and waited, but I didn't respond.

"You'd be doing me a favor," he said. "It has been ages since I've spoken German to someone face-to-face—spoken German to anyone at all. It would be quite nice to have a new friend to talk to."

I turned to face him. A friend, he'd said, and I nearly repeated him. "I would like that as well," I confessed, unable to stop myself from smiling openly now. We shook on the deal, and I bowed slightly in a formal way as I said, "Nice to meet you."

I went to Herr Weill's on Monday, Wednesday, and Friday afternoons. During our early conversations, it was a relief to land on his doorstep after six hours in a school where no one understood anything about me. My silence, my inability to grasp the very words being said in class, including my own name—mispronounced by the teacher taking the roll. The pungent food I brought for lunch that I ate with my hands. My solitary play at recess that usually involved creative projects with flowers, rocks, branches collected from the patch of wilderness on the edge of the playground. My need for expression took on nonverbal forms in those thirty minutes of freedom outdoors. I contributed nothing to the class discussions, and understood almost nothing as well, except during our math hour (what a short hour), my favorite subject, that universal language. Math and art, the only things I cared about. After these exhausting days, I'd walk the mile of country road to Herr Weill's tidy brick house, and it mattered that he always seemed pleased to see me.

Before I'd go up the walkway that perfectly bisected his perfectly manicured lawn, I'd always straighten my coat, tuck in my shirt, and inspect my shoes. He'd greet me in a suit and wing-tipped loafers, hold out his right hand for a handshake while his left arm was kept behind his back, like he was greeting a dignitary. His wispy white hair was always parted in the middle in an unwavering line from which thin strands were combed toward his ears. When those strands would flop as he was talking excitedly, shaking his head and index finger while making a point, he'd simply smooth his hair back down once he'd said his piece, that meridian reemerging just so. He had an unfussy home: no phone, sturdy furniture, lots of these framed silhouette paintings hanging on the walls. He'd set out tea and bread, cheese, and meats, and he always made me a to-go box to bring home to my mother. He was well regarded in town, and so my parents quickly warmed to the idea of these meetings, and especially the free English lessons. Whenever I asked my parents a question about English, they'd say, "That's one to remember for your professor." Herr Weill and I would usually meet for about two hours. My mother didn't have to worry about finding a sitter or some inexpensive after-school activity for me three days a week. Herr Weill was a blessing, she always said. Father wasn't particularly religious, but he agreed. Herr Weill was a blessing.

We worked through a basic English textbook that had a cartoon of a red schoolhouse with a big sun shining down actual rays of wavy lines, something any preschooler could have drawn, if he had no imagination. We sat with this workbook for an hour and spent the rest of the time speaking German. At first, I was surprised by how much I had to say. With both my parents spending long hours at work cleaning the chemistry lab by day and applying to training programs at night, and with no one to talk to in my neighborhood or at school, I had filled my days with so much silence that my time with Herr Weill was an unexpected outpouring.

I told him about the first time I saw West Berlin on Christmas Eve, and how I hid under my bed when I heard loud explosions that I thought were bombs, never having seen fireworks. I explained that the Zoological Garden on the way to the American Consulate was one of the saddest places I'd seen with my own eyes, and no living creatures should be forced to be caged up in a big cold city on account of our fascination and fear, which was no crime of theirs. I told him the line at the American Consulate was much longer than the one to get a picture with a panda by a long shot. At this, he laughed, finally.

I told him the wall seemed like it was everywhere, and the only thing I liked about it was those points you could touch that were covered in graffiti where people expressed a desire to overcome it. I'd fantasized about drawing fake stairs on its canvas, scrawling messages across painted paper airplanes or writing notes grasped in the claws of charcoal doves. Herman wanted to sketch a wind that could ascend those heights, but only managed to paint a few circles radiating out from where someone dared chip away at the concrete so it seemed that this slight crack might pulse, expand, crumble the whole thing. I confessed that I had also chipped off a tiny kernel using the knife that Ismail carried around ever since his father got beat up for being a foreigner.

Herr Weill didn't reveal very much that first day but opened up just to tell me he had been a refugee once, too, and had left home when he was a teenager because a war scattered his whole family. He spoke slowly and said little, but it was also an outpouring, I could tell. From then on, we talked often about these things, like conflict, violence, war, fleeing from it and the way it makes you tired whether you're running or still. We talked about scars, invisible and visible, instant and latent ones, all real. How hard it is not to keep losing things because of conflict, even once it's far away, miles or years away, and yet, how life fills up with other things all the while. At the end of that visit, he said, "It's a relief to be able to chat with someone around here about something other than Chuck Long," whom I'd never even heard of anyway.

The second time I visited Herr Weill, he gave me a leather journal so I would always have someone to talk to, if only the blank page. I wrote in German so that I could show it to Herr Weill if he ever asked to see it. I was always jotting down questions, notes about my life, about the things I'd encountered and wanted to think about, conversations that were ultimately reflections of what I longed to say and hear.

Li is from China. I've been sitting next to her in the back of the room ever since last week when we were the only people in the class without costumes for Halloween. She told me a secret, her family fled from the first country, and she asked me if I knew what she meant and I did. I told her I even knew what it meant to flee from the second country, and also to leave the third country, and that made her smile. She has a pretty smile. And she's really good at drawing. And geography. Maybe because she saw me writing in this journal, she gave me a box of pens today. She always has these nice pens she draws with that have little pandas on them. She gave me a whole box. How did she know I love pandas? Her English is worse than mine. When she handed me the pens, she said something like, "Your book." I tried to say, "Thanks, pandas are my favorite animals," but she didn't respond. Maybe underneath, it really went like this, or could have:

Me: How's everything?

Li: I'm fine, how are you?

Me: I'm fine. I've just been writing in this journal that my best friend gave me.

Li: What are you writing about?

Me: Oh just about life and love and things like that.

Li: Wow! I brought you pens so you can keep writing in your book.

Me: Thanks, pandas are my favorite animals!

Li: Mine, too!

Me: I'll dedicate this journal to you.

Li: I'd like that very much.

Later, I will try to tell Li that Heir Weill is taking me to the college library. It will be closed for Veteran's Day, but he has a "ritual" to go every year the day before on November 10. He thinks I might like it there, too.

Every November 10, Herr Weill would go to the college library to see what he called his German collection. Before we met, this was the only German he heard all year. He'd read German books out loud, and it was the only German he spoke all year, too. Herr Weill and I took a bus to the library. The roof of the bus had these little gold stars painted onto it, and I thought that was a fine touch. Unlike in Berlin, you could look up at night from any point in this town and see the stars anyway, but still, it was nice to be reminded of a clear night sky on a cold, overcast morning.

Herr Weill knew everyone at the library, and they all came over to say hi and see how he was doing. He introduced me to the research librarians and other staff. They took us to a very small room made of glass that reminded me of an elevator I'd once seen in Berlin. The room had two chairs in it and shelves for books. He gave the research librarian a stack of bits of paper with numbers and letters, and about a half hour later, the librarian rolled a cart over to our little room. The cart was full of books, maps, newspapers, photographs, most of them dusty as if they hadn't been touched all year.

We spent the whole day there with these items. So we could keep up our energy, Herr Weill snuck in breakfast, lunch sandwiches, a snack, and a light supper. I wrote down everything I could about what I saw in our glass room, because it was such a standout day. I saw:

- Café Elektric, *a silent film with Marlene Dietrich and with no ending because it is said to be lost. Herr Weill thinks the end was later lost in the war because that's the nature of war, to leave stories incomplete and rob us of our resolutions (we also listened to Marlene Dietrich sing in* Blue Angels)

- The Threepenny Opera *by his "namesake by coincidence," Kurt Weill. The song was about mercy being more important than justice and Herr Weill said he listened to it every year to see if he'd come any closer to deciding whether or not this was true, and if it was true, what it required of him or what it eased in him, so he said.*

- *Poems by the poet Rilke*

- *A few pages of* Zen in the Art of Archery, *which Herr Weill had been reading a few pages at a time for years, each year. We took turns reading aloud. He said Zen doesn't believe in language, so it's best to give the pages space, months, years to breathe. He folded over the top, a tiny bend marking where we would pick up next November.*

- *News clips from November 10, 1938, because of the treacherous anniversary of Kristallnacht. Herr Weill says it's important to acknowledge an anniversary, even the ones that mark tragedy. This was around the time he left Germany and became a refugee, which I can tell he doesn't like to speak about. He said very little about 1938 except that some things we can't help but to remember, and some we must struggle to forget. I forgot to ask him which things are which.*

- *Old maps and new ones because Herr Weill said that the borders can change on you, so you have to keep watch, keep checking in. Through the maps, I learned some more about Herr Weill and my old home:*

  - *Herr Weill was born in 1920, not in Berlin but in a suburb. By the time he was two months old, the city had grown at least three times because someone moved some lines on a map. So he was born just outside of Berlin and grew up in Berlin, having lived in the same house all his childhood. I saw the old map of Germany in 1919 and in 1920. He called it something else, Weimar.*

  - *He pointed out the borders of the Jewish Ghetto that he said had walls of its own when Germany was called something else, Third Reich, but he didn't call it that himself, he said.*

  - *We looked at a map of Germany after WWII with Berlin in the eastern part of the country. This was before the USSR built the wall, but still there was West Berlin with borders around it, a floating dot in the communist bloc. Herr Weill said, "It's a very uneasy thing to live life surrounded by enemies." I knew this to be true.*

○ *A satellite map outlining the wall built in 1961. From this point of view, it had none of the order I always associated with the wall.*

○ *On a modern map of West Berlin, I pointed out where our studio was situated in the shadow of the wall on the western side, which looked the same as the shadow that fell on the East. I pointed out where Herman and Ismail had lived. I also found the general location of our playground, and also where I liked to sit by the Spree and watch the boats when I was in the East and where I liked to sit by the Spree and watch the boats in the West just like I liked to watch the boats when we went on vacation to the banks of Lake Tana.*

I always remember the way Herr Weill quoted me back to myself after that day, saying, "You say you lived with your family 'in the shadow of the wall on the western side, which looked the same as the shadow that fell on the East. In this, you have pointed out the main aspect of a wall that these damn architects never seem to grasp: no matter which side you're on, its shadow is cast on you." He'd say it at random times and reflect on those words in a way that made me feel understood.

At the end of our visit to the college library, Herr Weill wished me a happy eve of Armistice Day, his favorite holiday marking the end of World War I, a "war to end all wars, a day that for a moment must have seemed to promise eternal peace, for a while." I asked, "Why celebrate a day that was a lie? There was no armistice to end all wars," but Herr Weill replied, "Even if a promise isn't kept, it doesn't mean there has been a lie." He said we'd do this again next year, and being let in to this annual ritual gave me the feeling we'd be friends for a long time. Before I left, Herr Weill invited me and my parents to lunch at his home on November 11, but I told him my father didn't have the day off and my mother wanted me to help mend the winter clothes we'd been given while we were still wearing our fall clothes.

November 14, sunny, freezing, so cold that recess is getting shorter so we've been playing inside. I started to pass notes to Li in the back of the room:

Monday: Do you like me? Yes, No, Maybe

> *Li answered by drawing a doodle of a cat sleeping on a chair.*

Tuesday: Want to play after study time? Yes, No, Maybe (circle one)

> *Li answered by drawing a tic-tac-toe board and putting an x in the middle.*

Wednesday: No note (playing it cool)

Thursday: Would you like to share my juice box today?

> *Li drew a sun with sunglasses on it!*

Friday: Can we play tomorrow in the park?

> *Li wrote the words to the Pledge of Allegiance.*

I couldn't tell if Li and I were growing closer or missing each other. As for my other friends, Ismail and Herman left Germany just before I did, and the only letter I wrote was never forwarded, just returned unopened, wrong address. I couldn't write my friends back home because they were angry that I left and accused me of abandoning them. Though I barely talked to Li, I longed to know her better.

I brought my heartache to Herr Weill, tentatively. I eased into the subject, asking Herr Weill, "When I first met you, didn't you say there was a woman you looked at once with longing?" He lifted his brow and revealed that, sure, he'd loved a woman once. They were neighbors in Berlin. He was shy, she was shy. He'd carry her groceries, walk her to school sometimes, tried to show her he was a dependable rock in her life, and he had it all planned out in his mind: when he graduated from high school, started a job, and had enough money to take her out in style, then he'd ask her to dinner. But the war happened, and it didn't end in time. They both walked into the war, never reconnecting. She was always good to him. Her name was Margareta.

I asked him, "If you never married her, did you ever marry anyone else?"

"Almost once, but it fell apart. Then another time almost, but it slipped through my fingers. That seemed like as many chances as I was going to get. But I every so often wonder about Margareta, just like I wonder about many things from back home that eluded me," he admitted.

"Do you regret not pursuing her?" I asked him.

"You see," he said, "one always regrets a lack of courage. In one form or another, that's probably the only kind of regret anyone ever has. She taught me that."

"So you tried to find her again later?" I pressed, testing my own feelings about Li against his answers and experience.

"No, I haven't tried to find her yet," he said. I didn't feel the need to tell him the obvious, that forty-five years seemed long enough to wait. But I knew there were risks in revisiting the past, unintended consequences of opening certain doors. I sensed that's what held him back. It wasn't fear, he didn't harbor that. I guessed he traded hope for security, and I could understand where he was coming from, which made me even more upset. I decided that it was my turn to show Herr Weill something new, that some risks were always worthwhile even if they might throw wide open our vaulted pasts and hearts. I came up with a strategy to win Li, ASAP, but also to give a certain lost optimism back to Herr Weill: I called the plan Operation Panda Margareta.

I talked to Herr Weill about it, and he seemed charmed; he understood that something as monumental as Operation Panda Margareta would need to be dramatic, carefully planned and very carefully implemented. The next time I saw him I showed him my idea, which he thought seemed adequately heroic:

OPERATION PANDA MARGARETA

9:15: Sneaking into the Principal's Office while Principal is out for his daily smoke/walk

9:16: Play Jackson Five's "ABC" over the PA

9:17: Read a poem for Li

9:19: Run!

I worked on the plan on my own, especially writing the poem, which took time since my English was still halting. In a couple of weeks, when I was leaving school to visit Herr Weill and go over last-minute details for Operation Panda Margareta, recite the poetry, test out the cassette player he'd loaned me, and go over the book I'd checked out from the library on operating a PA system, I noticed Thomas Henry—sweet, quiet farm kid—come down the front steps of the school, walk up to Li and, without saying a thing, put his arm around her in a familiar way, like he'd certainly done it before. Behind his ear, he had a panda pen, and my heart was sinking. I fumbled for the poem in my pocket, and I almost did what I had meant to do, read these words to Li, declare my feelings. When Thomas and Li walked by, I tried to catch Li's gaze, but I couldn't quite keep it.

I stopped writing in my notebook after this, and just before winter break, Li began sitting with Thomas and his friends up by the front of the room. I joined a soccer club and cut back on my visits to Herr Weill's. I made all kinds of excuses, but the truth is really as my English improved, other barriers came down, too. I was discovering more about my classmates; it turned out they also found it fun to watch the magic tricks that Benny the crossing guard practiced on his breaks and also liked playing in the cleared fields surrounding town. They pranked me by teaching me dirty words but telling me the wrong definition (for about a week, I thought *cabbage* was an insult, *artichoke* a sin to say). I pranked them by showing them sophisticated, "worldly" ways to dance and walk and roller-skate that were ridiculous and hilarious and got us all kicked out of a few establishments.

So in this way, Herr Weill and I drifted apart, allowed ourselves to become somewhat untied from each other, and let the ebb and flow of life move us along our own paths, just as he intended. I'd still go by from time to time, after chatting at the community center and making plans to meet some weeks until eventually, with weekend matches to play, I stopped going to those Sunday potlucks, too. When I did come over, Herr Weill would put out meats, cheeses, breads as always, and I allowed myself to imagine he did this whether I came or not, set out this spread every afternoon, that he wasn't going out of his way for me on these haphazard visits. By the spring, my parents decided it was time for us to move again, this time toward something: a new job for my father. A better job not too far away. And so we packed our bags again, I hoped for the last time.

Herr Weill and I wrote letters for the first few months after this, but then, I guess I just couldn't keep up, or just didn't. The letters piled up, four unanswered ones from Herr Weill that I'd only read quickly, meant to answer but hadn't, life becoming something else by now.

We nearly met again, almost, just after November 9, 1989, when suddenly and unexpectedly, the Berlin Wall fell. My first thought upon hearing the news was about where Ismail and Herman were, and whether they could reclaim our lost soccer balls. My second thought was, did Herr Weill see the news and what did he think/ do/say? I tried to look up Herr Weill in the phone book, but he still didn't have a number listed, so telling my parents what I wanted to do, they reluctantly let me take the car to visit him the next day, November 10. I managed to get to the library before it closed. I went to Herr Weill's usual desk, but he had left. When I asked, the librarian said Herr Weill had come by for just a short visit, and I'd missed him by hours. I requested that old copy of *Zen in the Art of Archery* and saw he'd gone through a few more pages, advanced six unobtrusive folds since the time we'd read from this book.

I retraced a path I'd walked so many times, driving that road through the fields and wooded brush. I drove right by his house at first, looking for a large home, circling back, puzzling over how modest it actually was. The paint was faded, but the mailbox was new. The lawn was strewn with leaves, some soggy and patted down and some fresh atop that cover, like he hadn't cleared the yard in weeks, maybe all season. I wondered if he was sick, if he needed help with chores, maybe an old hurt had returned, an old haunting, maybe the ghost of the past had found him again. It was too late to ring the bell, I told myself. It would have been awkward to visit unannounced then, and I realized I hadn't worked out what I'd have said, anyway. I couldn't find the words somehow, not because I didn't know them, but because they didn't exist. Maybe I didn't need them, maybe a gesture would say it all. I found myself clearing his lawn with my bare hands of all those messy leaves and filling up his mulch bin. I then stayed to pull the tiny weeds that just sprouted up in the cracks on his pathway leading to his porch, which already had an American flag flying for Armistice Day ("Armistice Day, flags display," Herr Weill once said). Next I drove into the quiet town, the shops on Main closed, yet all with bright red, white, and blue banners hanging. I passed my old school, the community center, circled back down by the college, saw the movie theater and the roller rink, each taking on an aura of reverence that a quiet holiday brings.

I thought I might look up Li and see if her family had managed to stay still in her second country. She'd have been sixteen, a junior in high school, but I never got the courage for that, either. I imagined she was getting ready to go to homecoming with Thomas, maybe thinking about buying him a boutonniere and he asking her what color her dress was so he could find the right corsage. As I was filling up the gas tank to make the trip back, I wondered if I'd regret not looking for Li, and I knew I'd regret not having stopped in to visit Herr Weill, our friendship that I'd once thought would last for years already somehow in the past. At least before heading home, I'd left him a note, simply my address atop the first page in the journal he'd once given me and that I still carried around from

time to time. In the margin of the torn-out page, I wrote: 11/10/89
– *To my first friend in my fourth country on the event of the end of the
wall. A heartfelt and happy Armistice Day.*

Then, in faded ink and smudged lettering:

October 15, 1983:

To Herr Weill: Thanks for this journal. It's terrific.

*To Journal: Welcome to my life! Herr Weill is my first friend
here so far. We have some things in common and some not:*

*My favorite food: wurst with kraut and mustard, also doro wat or
kitfo with injera.*

> ○ *Herr Weill's favorite: schnitzel because his mother used to
> make it and it is "comfort food."*

My favorite movie: Casablanca, *ever since they played it at the
American Consulate because it was about refugees.*

> ○ *Herr Weill's favorite:* Casablanca*! He says it's a story about
> true friendship.*

*My favorite season: I hate the cold because of the way it makes you
cry, but I love reading next to a fire.*

> ○ *Herr Weill's favorite season: He loves the vigor of the cold,
> but he hates the snow, too mushy when it melts.*

So what else can this mean but that we both love the fall?

The Street Sweep

Getu stood in front of his mirror struggling to perfect a Windsor knot. He pulled the thick end of his tie through the loop, but the knot unraveled in his hands. He tried again, and again he failed. Did he really need the tie? He guessed it would probably be easier to persuade the guards at the Sheraton to let him in with one. And even then . . . .

But he couldn't work out the steps, so Getu put the necktie in his pocket and decided to try his luck without it. Sitting at the edge of his mattress, he waited for the hour to pass. (He didn't want to arrive too early, too eager.) His straw mattress was on the floor in the corner, and it was covered with all of his clothes, which earlier that evening he had tried on, considered, ruled out, reconsidered, tossed aside before choosing a blue shirt (stained under the arms, but he'd conceal the stains with his jacket) and black pants. Until that day, Getu thought this was an adequate wardrobe, fairly nice for a street sweeper, but he had noticed even his best pants were worn at the hem, so he brought them to his mother.

She was busy chopping onions, and her red hands and tear-ful eyes gave Getu pause. He didn't want to add to her burden, but he needed her help. "Momma," he said, and she immediately responded, "Later," and walked right past him to the garden that was nestled into the several paces that separated the gate from the small home.

He thumbed the rebellious threads that seemed to be disinte-grating in his fingers. "Please, Momma. This stitching is coming apart." She didn't look up from her vegetable garden where she was picking some hot peppers, so he pressed on. "I need to look nice for Mr. Jeff's farewell party."

"Ah, Mr. Jeff," she turned to face Getu and would have thrown up her hands except for the peppers resting on her lifted apron. "Again with Mr. Jeff," she groaned.

"I have to see him. It's his last night in Addis Ababa. And he's been so good to me," Getu explained, following his mother back to the kitchen that was softly lit by the sun filtering through the thinning corrugated plastic roof.

She called over her shoulder, "Has he been good to you? What has Mr. Jeff actually done for you?"

Getu hesitated, then said, "Mr. Jeff told me he has something for me." He'd have said more but she was barely paying attention to him, focused on wiping off the peppers on her apron, splitting them in half, and taking out all the seeds. "Momma," he said.

"I heard you, it's just . . . what is it you imagine he has for you?" Getu didn't dare honestly answer that question, his mother's rid-icule primed for the slightest provocation. Ever since Jeff Johnson invited him to the party, Getu couldn't stop himself from guessing what this something might be. Over their months of friendship, Jeff Johnson had told Getu how important Getu was to him, how his organization could use a young man like Getu, and what a brilliant, keen head Getu had on his shoulders. Getu's hopes had soared as he pictured the good job he'd surely be offered. In this moment, he nearly told his mother all about the new, stable life he'd imagined, the freedom from worry that would come from the big paycheck he'd surely bring in, which would be so liberating now that the government seizure of land was creeping closer neighborhood by neighborhood. Even the Tedlus had lost their home just a month ago, and they only lived five blocks away. But Getu simply replied, "I just want to say goodbye to Mr. Jeff."

"Getu, if this Mr. Jeff really wants you at his party, then he won't care what you wear."

"But, Momma, it's at the Sheraton," Getu whispered.

"At the Sheraton, did you say?" She turned and stared at him with raised eyebrows and a sorry look in her eyes. "It's at the Sheraton?" Her tone started high, then fell with Getu's spirits.

"Do you really think this man wants you there? At the Sheraton? He invited you to a party at the Sheraton? Only a man who has spent every day here having his shoes licked and every door flung open would be so unaware as to invite a boy like you to the Sheraton. To the Sheraton! Who is this Mr. Jeff?"

Getu didn't have the courage to reply, so she continued. "Let me tell you. He comes, is chauffeured to one international office after another, and at the end of the night, he goes to the fancy clubs on Bole Road, feasts, drinks, passes out, wakes up, then calls his chauffer who has slept lightly with his phone placed right by his head and with the ringer turned up high so as not to miss a call from the likes of Mr. Jeff and disappoint the likes of Mr. Jeff. And then one day this Mr. Jeff invites my boy to a party at the Sheraton. At the Sheraton! They'll never let you in, of course. The Sheraton? Oh, I could go on about this Mr. Jeff."

Getu's mother had long ago formed her opinion about the Mr. Jeffs of the world. She had seen men and women like Jeff Johnson breeze through the country for decades, an old pattern. She'd kept her distance from these eager aid workers flown over for short stints with some big new NGO, this or that agency, such and such from who knows where. They appeared in her neighborhood, gave her surveys to fill out, and offered things she reluctantly accepted (vaccines and vitamins), things she quite happily pawned (English language books and warm clothing), and things at which she turned up her nose (genetically modified seeds and antimicrobial soap). Without fail, the Mr. Jeffs shaped then reshaped her neighborhood in new ways year in, year out. She compared them to the floods that washed out the roads in the south of the country each rainy season, carving fresh paths behind them, a cyclical force of change and re-creation. Each September after the rainy season ended and the new recruits from Western universities came to Ethiopia, she was known to have said, "And now let the storms begin."

"Momma," Getu said softly, snapping his mother out of her thoughts. "This is a really important night for me."

"I know you think that. But you're eighteen, and you haven't seen enough yet to know what I know."

"Eighteen here is like seventy-five anywhere else," he rebutted.

"Can't I talk sense into you? Is a mother's love and wisdom no match for whatever hold Mr. Jeff has over you?"

"But, Momma, we need him. He'll help us save our home," Getu said, finally owning up to that hope that had started as a little seed and sprouted and taken root and now seemed as sturdy as an acacia.

After a pause that would have been enough for her to turn the idea around in her head more than once, she asked, "Do you think he can do that?" She didn't believe in the Mr. Jeffs, who seemed predictable by now, but she knew Getu was full of surprises.

Getu held out the clothes he needed mended, and she took them cautiously. Getu followed her to the living room and watched her sew expertly. As she moved the needle through the thin fabric, she flicked her wrist and mumbled the long list of chores she was putting on hold to take care of this task. Getu found his mood lifting as he saw her expertise with the needle and thread. His clothes looked almost new. When she'd finished, Getu took them gratefully from her, though he felt her resistance still, for she held her tight grip even as he pulled them away.

Anyone could see the Sheraton was palatial, seemed literally ten times bigger than the presidential palace, and there were several reasons why. Of course there was the size; the Sheraton was sprawling. Also, the presidential palace was gated and tucked into a forested acreage in the city, so the structure peeked out from between the iron fencing and shrubbery. It was impossible to *behold*. But you could *behold* the Sheraton looming above all else on a hill in the city center. At night, it was spotlighted from below, and with the neighborhoods around it empty or without electricity because of frequent power shortages, the Sheraton, alone with its invisible generators, illuminated that part of town each night, every night, no fail. Most importantly, the Sheraton was exclusive but not exclusionary. Some were allowed in while others were not, and this selective accessibility gave it more mystique than the palace, which was completely off limits to all but the president and his close coterie. The Sheraton created a sense of hope when it opened its arms to the few, and so occupied the ambitions of many. Inside, there were cafés, restaurants, a sprawling pool, and enough amenities to fill a hefty foldout brochure, including a multi-DJ nightclub called the Gaslight. The Sheraton was an unmistakable presence in the city, an isle of exclusive luxury that didn't quite touch down.

Walking the long road from his home to the Sheraton, Getu carried his jacket, tie in pocket. He walked slowly so as not to get too sweaty by the time he arrived, and as he walked, he practiced all the ways he'd ask Mr. Jeff for his just reward. As soon as he had the courage, he'd gently bring up the matter of the job he felt was due to him. As he made his way through town, he passed burdened mules, cars trapped in traffic jams, old men and women who preferred trudging along the road to waiting for the crowded buses. Young men sat on street curbs getting stoned on chat, which they languidly chewed with nothing better to do than watch the slow-moving yet frenetic scenes drift by.

When Getu approached the foot of the hill that led up to the Sheraton, the buzz of the city quieted. Around this barren land, bureaucrats had erected yellow and green fences of corrugated tin to keep out any unwanted men, women, dogs, cats, and others they considered strays. It started with a single law: if a house in Addis Ababa is less than four stories tall, then your land can and will be seized. To keep your home, build! Whether there were new investors lined up or not, land across town was being exuberantly razed to make way for the new. Neighborhood by neighborhood, stucco houses vanished; makeshift tent homes made of cloth and rags and wood were swept away; moon-houses—put up at night by leaning tin siding against a wall—were tossed aside by morning.

"Who has a four-story house?" Getu's mother had shouted frantically when she first heard about the law. "They'll get rid of everything, except maybe the Sheraton," she had said.

Getu said, "Be calm, I'll take care of it. We'll make it work."

"What will we do? Of course we'll move wherever these powers that be put us. I hear they're pushing people to the outskirts of town, but how will I get to work then? I was born in this house, and why don't they just leave me alone to die here, too?"

"I'm going to handle it, Momma. You'll see. I'll make you proud," Getu said, stepping close to his mother and rubbing her back.

"Lord, this son of mine," Getu's mother said into her folded hands.

"There's a way. I can get a new job," Getu assured.

"You sweep sidewalks. What could you do with your broom and your dustbin? Anyway, who's to say that today they tell us to build a four-story house, tomorrow they won't demand the Taj Mahal. Just let it go."

"But, Momma— "

"What food crossed my lips when I was pregnant to end up with a dreamer for a son? Didn't I forgo meat and dairy each holiday? Did I overlook butter one Wednesday by mistake, or milk some absentminded Friday?"

"I could get a job with one of the international organizations. We could build a dozen four-story houses."

"Every single week, did I not attend church?"

"Mother, you don't understand. I have a new friend."

"Did I stare too long at someone cursed with an evil eye?"

"I've helped him. He'll help me when the time comes. Mr. Jeff is a friend of mine."

Up through the swept-clean land, up the hill, along the winding road, Getu walked to the Sheraton and, before he was in the sight line of the guards, put on his jacket and smoothed his shirt, the necktie still in a bundle in his right-hand pocket. Getu also brought a small wrapped gift, a map of the city that he bought at a tourist shop in Mercato. Getu circled where his house was on this map, and on the back he wrote his address and phone number should Mr. Jeff want to visit.

Though the sun hadn't set yet, the spotlights in front of the Sheraton were already on, illuminating the driveways and pathways outside the hotel, every inch meticulously landscaped with palms, hedges, and blooming flowers punctuating the long curving roads leading to the five-story building and its various wings and annexes. Getu took a deep breath and stared at the vast space. He tried to visualize walking up to the guard, throwing a casual smile, saying a quick, "Hello, how are you?" Maybe he'd affect an accent so the guards might mistake him for one of the diaspora who lived abroad and returned with foreign wealth and connections and, it seemed, ease.

He took his first step down the hotel pathway. The concrete beneath his feet was spotless, as if it had just been scrubbed clean. "Remarkable. They even kept out the soot and the dust," Getu said to himself.

When he reached the guard stand, Getu mumbled a greeting to the two guards. One of the guards, the short one, walked up to Getu, and the other, quite tall, stepped back and began to read the paper. The guard in front of Getu was dressed in a khaki-colored suit and wore a black top hat with gold braided trim. He looked around Getu, to his left, his right, almost through him, it seemed. "Are you here alone?" the guard asked.

"Yes, I'm here to meet my friend Mr. Jeff for his going-away party." Getu tried to hold himself tall. "He invited me."

"A party, huh? Here?" The guard swayed onto his tiptoes and tilted his head back, and so managed to look down on Getu, despite being a couple inches shorter than him. "Where are you from?"

"I'm from Lideta. I have cousins in America, so that explains my accent." He was from Lideta, a small, modest neighborhood that rested in the shadow of the Lideta Cathedral. The rest was lies.

"You call him Mr. Jeff?" The guard considered this. "Are you his servant?"

Getu shook his head. He wasn't convincing them. He'd have to think fast, and fiddled with the necktie in his pocket. If only he had stopped along the way to get help putting it on. "I am, as Mr. Jeff says, his man on the street, his ear to the ground. I help with his work."

"What kind of work?" As the guard walked around Getu, his heels clicked rhythmically against the ground like a ticking watch.

"NGO work," Getu said, and seeing the guard's eyebrows rise, he kept on. "International NGO work," Getu stressed. He had the guard's attention.

The guard looked Getu up and down closer than before: Getu's worn clothes, his short rough fingernails, the quality of the calluses on his hands, the tan lines at his wrists, the red highlights in his hair, his muscular form, the freckles on his cheeks, the cracked skin of his lips. "What do you do for him? A farmer, maybe? A herder? Are you his laborer?"

This was taking a turn for the worse, and Getu scrambled to get back on course. "I help my uncles in the countryside a few times a year. A man who is at ease in the city and the countryside, Mr. Jeff says. I'm his versatile aide, Mr. Jeff calls it."

"But what do you do?"

"He asks me questions about local things, and I answer them."

"Does it pay well?" The guard's skepticism mingled with blossoming interest.

"It will. He says I'm important. The exact English word is *invaluable*."

"*Valuable?*"

"*In-valuable*," Getu corrected, thinking of how to steer the conversation back to those big closed doors.

"But why you? Why are you *in-valuable*? You don't look like you went to Lycee or the British school?"

He wished the guard would stop inspecting his clothes like this, like they were his calling card. If only he'd had another way to identify himself. "Just think of me as a scholar. I mean, schooling-wise, I'm mostly self-taught, but I was accepted to American university. The fellowship wouldn't cover all the expenses, but this impressed Mr. Jeff enough when I told him."

"That can't be true."

"It is," Getu said. And it was. Getu was still staring impatiently now at the door of the Sheraton, held open for what he guessed was a French family, and he talked faster. "My mother says it's like a disease, but I'll read anything. Math, science, history, literature, law, politics. And I remember it, too. Mr. Jeff says it's a near-miracle."

"Yeah right," the short guard said, looking over his shoulder and taking the day's paper out of his partner's hands.

"You read English, of course," he said to Getu sarcastically.

"Of course," Getu said back. "English, French, Amharic, German—"

The guard put his hand up. "Just read this first paragraph." He pointed to the story on the top left side of the paper, then watched as Getu read. A few seconds later, the guard snatched back the paper. His hat slipped a little, and the guard lifted it back up, his attention fixed on Getu's eyes. "What did it say?"

Getu recited word for word the story about the new round of World Bank loans for modernizing agriculture. "That can't be!" The tall guard came closer to see what was going on. "This boy's like Solomon, watch," said the short guard as he put the paper back in front of Getu. "Read this paragraph," he ordered.

Without needing to be told, Getu read, looked away a few moments later, and recited the column about farmland rented out to foreign corporations.

"It's a trick," the tall guard said. "No way you memorized it just now."

"He works for an international NGO," the short guard explained.

"Can you let me in? I need to go to my boss's, my friend's, Mr. Jeff's party. It would be rude of me not to, and he is an important man." Getu said this impulsively, not sure if it was true.

"What was his name? What's your name?" the tall guard asked.

"My name is Getu Abebe. His name is Mr. Jeff. Jeff Johnson. Jefferson Johnson to be precise. He introduced himself to me as Jeff Johnson, but out of respect—"

"He's with an NGO. We can let this guy in," said the short guard.

"Is he on the list?" the tall guard asked.

"I don't know about a list. I am Getu Abebe."

"Wait here," the tall guard said, and as he turned and pulled open the tall glass doors of the hotel, a gust of cool air sent a chill down Getu's neck as he watched the guard disappear inside.

Getu had met Jeff Johnson six months before by a pub across the street from the UN agencies. Every evening at six, the pub filled with aid workers, both locals and foreigners, but mostly foreigners.

When Getu was sweeping the sidewalk one warm evening, Jeff Johnson and a group of other Americans stood outside smoking and talking loudly. Jeff Johnson called out to Getu and asked him to settle an old argument about the extent that "everyday people" benefit from aid given to corrupt governments. The parking lot attendant heard this question, turned, and walked quietly and quickly away. The bouncer stepped inside, making a general gesture of being cold in the 70-degree weather. But Getu, who'd never had an audience like this before, spoke loudly. Jeff Johnson and his friends fell quiet, leaned in, and listened attentively to each word.

Jeff Johnson pointed out that as a street sweeper, Getu must see a lot in the city, and Getu said, "Not only see, but smell, hear, and clear." Jeff Johnson and his friends leaned in even closer. Someone asked Getu, "What do you feel would be the most meaningful change for people your age in your neighborhood?" Getu thought about it and said, "It's a long way to school from my neighborhood, and so I'm self-educated. Many of my friends also forgo school because the bus is too unreliable." Jeff Johnson and his circle told Getu what a terrible shame this was, and the more they shook their heads, the more empowered Getu felt. Jeff Johnson and his circle asked for details, exact locations, the number of people who would benefit, community impact, scalability. A few weeks later, a private free shuttle suddenly began stopping on Getu's block taking passengers from around where Getu lived to the closest grammar school. Getu could hardly believe his eyes, like he'd conjured it up himself with his fingertips. Jeff Johnson saw Getu soon after the shuttle began running and listened as Getu praised the deed, which would make a big difference in the lives of his neighbors. "Team effort on this one," Jeff Johnson deflected. "You know, we could use a man like you in our organization. It's important to know what the man on the street thinks about what we do. You'd be an asset to us. Look how much you've already done." The words rung in his ears all that night as Getu imagined a new life for himself with those new friends, their salaries, their style, their access, their influence.

That experience left an impression on Getu, and the relationship that developed over daily discussions outside the pub during Jeff Johnson's cigarette breaks was the most significant in Getu's life so far, Getu thought. Through their discussions, Getu was able to magically engender new textbooks for the local library; a water well near the contaminated stream where he'd often seen people drink; a seminar series on prenatal care, which Getu hadn't suggested, but had approved. After each new program, Jeff Johnson would tell Getu, "We're a dream team. We'll be running this show in five years." Getu couldn't imagine not saying goodbye to Jeff Johnson on his last day in Addis Ababa, and he trusted Jeff Johnson—with all his powers—would come through for him somehow, now that Getu was the one in need.

Getu was still waiting for the tall guard to return when he caught a snippet of conversation between two women and realized one seemed familiar to him. "I wouldn't trust Jeff with my book collection," she'd said. "He'd probably end up giving it away." The young woman was pink with sunburn and was applying aloe to her shoulders.

"Or misplacing it all," said the other woman who was walking slowly while looking at herself in a compact and opening a tube of lip gloss.

"So then I don't know why you'd let him borrow your car," said the first woman, putting away her tube of gel.

"Because," mumbled her friend, who paused to apply the gloss then smiled into her compact. "But he does always mean well, that Jeff," she said, pursing her lips, walking up to the door of the Sheraton without casting a glance at the guard station.

Just as the short guard held open the door, Getu approached the woman with the pink sunburn, and he called out, "Madame!"

"No change, sorry, honey," the woman dismissed. The short guard heard this and shook his head; he knew Getu wasn't a beggar, and clearly disapproved of the woman's words, for regardless, she should have blessed Getu, invoked some higher kindness if her own did not compel her to give.

"Madame, it's me, Getu. I'm Mr. Jeff's aide. His man on the street. I think we met by the pub outside the UN."

The young woman looked at him for a moment, and said, "Of course, Getu." She leaned in to kiss him three times, as was the custom, but the spark of recognition never entered her eyes. Getu could smell the scent of the aloe gel, subtle, like a broken blade of grass.

"Madame, forgive me, but I don't know if I ever got your name," Getu said bowing slightly.

"It's Patricia," she said. "Pat. And this is a friend of mine, Lisa, Lis." She gestured toward the other woman, who also leaned in and kissed Getu on the cheek, left, right, left. The two women reached into their purses and pulled out their business cards, which Getu took, memorized, and put in his jacket pocket. Pat worked with a management consulting firm, Lis with a multilateral.

"We were just going to see Jeff now," Pat said to Getu.

"I wish I could join you. Mr. Jeff invited me to his farewell party, but the guards are asking a lot of questions," Getu said, trying to look inconvenienced but not desperate.

"Come with us," Lis said, then linked her arm with Getu's and boldly walked through the door, passing the guard, who smiled as Getu entered. Inside, Getu, Pat, and Lis were searched, and Pat and Lis tossed their bags on the scanner before walking through the metal detector.

Pat turned to him and said, "Entering the Sheraton always feels like going through airport security, don't you think?"

Getu nodded, but he had never been inside, nor had he flown, either. He wiped his shoes several times on the doormat as he stood by the scanner. The guard there asked him to take off his jacket and put it through the machine. He hadn't planned for this, and wished he had asked his mother to help wash away the stubborn sweat stains on his shirt. He took off the jacket using a rigid motion, keeping his elbows tucked into his body, then walked through security without swaying his arms. He put the jacket on again using the same constricted motions.

But Getu quickly forgot about his jacket or the stains. Such insignificant things could hardly compete with the opulent gilding, glass, and marble that surrounded him, and the colossal fountain in the center of the lobby. The polished clientele wore colorful clothes from West Africa and India, or the gray and black geometric shapes of New York or London. Getu inched as close as he could to Lis and Pat and followed them as they led him through a kind of abundance he'd never seen before. The air-conditioned lobby opened in front of him with its high archways, its shining floors, its multitude of rugs that would have had to be folded in quarters to fit in his bedroom. Overcome and transported into a world that seemed to swallow him whole, Getu couldn't sense himself.

Pat's loud laughter broke his trance, and she threw her arms around two tall men and a young Ethiopian woman. Getu was introduced and handed three new business cards from Pete from

DFID, Chuck from OECD, and Nardos from OHCHR, and he trailed the group, almost stepping on their heels as they made their way downstairs to the Gaslight.

The party was a blur at first. Pat declared she was going straight to the bar to start a tab, and the others followed, leaving Getu to wander on his own. After fifteen minutes, Getu found the man of the hour, and when he saw Getu, Jeff Johnson quickly came over, and shouted, "You made it! You came."

"Yes, of course. I said I'd come. It's your farewell," Getu said and embraced Jeff Johnson, who wore a gray suit, his dark brown hair shaggy and loose, a departure from his usual combed-back style. Getu noticed Jeff Johnson had his tie untied around his neck. "You couldn't tie it either?" Getu said.

"What?"

"Your tie—"

"Yeah, after a long last day, I had to loosen the grip, you know."

"Yes, mine's in my pocket," Getu said, and mimicked his host, throwing his tie around his neck and letting it hang loose like an untied scarf. Getu then took the small gift from his pocket, and handed it to Jeff Johnson, who seemed to appreciate the present. "I love maps," Jeff Johnson said, half-opening a crease, then folding it back up.

"That's my home, here," Getu said, unfolding it all the way, pointing to the circled spot. "It has been in my family a long time," he added, wondering if he'd still be living there the next time Jeff Johnson came to town, if there was a next time. He began to ease into his ask, saying, "I wish you could visit. I know we've talked about it—"

"I've really meant to," Jeff Johnson said, and put the map carefully in his pocket.

"Next time," Getu said, adding, "I might have to get you a new map then, though, with all the changes in the city."

"Yes, I bet when I see you again, you'll be living in one of those big new houses. I'm not worried about you, Getu."

"Really? I'm quite concerned—"

"Hope is the greatest asset a man can have, you know," Jeff Johnson said, then trailed off, distracted by a group who passed to wave hello. "Anyway, I really think with a little optimism a guy like you—intelligent, kind, driven, and articulate—can do anything he wants, if he puts his mind to it."

"Do you really think so, because—"

"Hey, Jeff, there you are!" Pat was standing with Lis, Nardos, and a tall red-haired man with square glasses. Jeff Johnson introduced Getu to Toni from AfDB, and others who made their way into and out of the discussion. Getu collected business cards from a roving editor, a strategic specialist, a starlet and her agent, a relief worker, and a freelance philanthropist.

"Can I buy you a drink?" Jeff Johnson asked Getu after a lull. Getu was about to direct the conversation back to his home, but talking over a drink seemed like the best approach.

"Oh, let me buy you one," Getu said taking out his wallet.

"Oh no, they're overpriced here," Jeff Johnson said, and flagged down the bartender. "Can't allow it."

"It's the Ethiopian way. You are a guest about to go! You must let me."

"Okay, if it's a cultural thing, I guess I'll have a beer," he said to the bartender. "Just a draft. Local." Getu ordered water. Jeff Johnson was absorbed in a heated debate, so when Getu got the bill, no one was paying attention when Getu realized the water cost more than the beer, and either way, he couldn't cover what he owed. Getu thought of his mother, and her insistence that Mr. Jeff's world was not his world, even if they shared a city code. Still, here he was in whatever world this was, and someone had to pay. He began counting his money discreetly under the bar; somehow he'd misjudged his cash by a factor of ten. Getu leaned toward the bartender, and without knowing what he was going to say, found himself whispering, "Can you put this on Miss, on Pat's tab? Patricia Walcott, Pat. She's getting this one." The bartender nodded without asking any questions, and like that, Getu wondered if once in, he was operating within a new system of trust. Whereas in his life, establishing those bonds required quite a lot, especially around money matters (too much to lose), here, an unfamiliar nonchalance seemed to permeate. He took a chance and ordered himself a beer, just one, on Pat's tab, too.

A fog machine was positioned in the corner of the room, and small spotlights and stage lights dotted the trance-like Gaslight with glimmering blue, purple, and white. The atmosphere disoriented Getu, and as soon as he walked away from the bar, he realized he'd lost Jeff Johnson again. Getu ran into a few people he had met in the past through Jeff Johnson, but for the most part, he walked around the party looking for the host, introducing himself to one guest after the next as "Mr. Jeff's man on the street," which others found endearing. He hopped from conversation to conversation, gathering business card after business card from employees of all kinds of organizations (GFAR, PEPFAR, ILRI, USAID, UNFPA, UNESCO, UNICEF, UNDP, UNECA, IDB, IFC, ICTSD, FAO, WIPO, OIE, WTPF), memorizing them, putting them in his pocket in careful order. He was pulled onto the dance floor as he followed Mr. Jeff's trail, dragged upstairs where he heard Jeff Johnson was by a firepit gorging himself on tibs, but Getu didn't find him there, either. From time to time, he touched the business cards in his pocket, played with the stack as he made his way through the maze of a hotel. He finally found Jeff Johnson by the swimming pool in the back, sitting with a group, and went over to his host. Just as he arrived, Jeff Johnson stood and announced it was almost time for him to go. The night had snuck by and Getu still hadn't asked after his job. He'd have to be direct, risk being awkward about it, or miss his shot completely.

Jeff Johnson said goodbye to his friends and left them at the pool, but Getu insisted he'd walk to the gate. Jeff Johnson said, "You've been a good friend to me, Getu. A gracious host, my man on the street. I'm lucky to have met you."

"Thank you very kindly. About that, I—"

"It's like I always say, we really could use a man like you on the team." Jeff Johnson spoke all his familiar lines.

"Then hire me," Getu said, pointing at himself and finally voicing what had been on his mind the entire night, if not their entire friendship. "Hire me."

Jeff Johnson laughed gently. "I know, right? Exactly. I wish I could."

"Then do!"

"Oh, Getu." Jeff Johnson looked at Getu, and seeing his serious face, he turned serious, too. "I'm sorry, did I give you the wrong . . . Did you think . . . ?" Getu listened very closely. Jeff Johnson took a step back, a look of clarity descended. "I think you've misunderstood somehow. I'm just a junior staffer, so obviously . . . ," he said as if that explained it. "I mean, of course I'm hoping this assignment will lead to a promotion, but you know . . ."

"But you know people. I'm counting on you," Getu said. His voice was tense though he tried to sound casual. If he'd misunderstood, hadn't he been misled?

"You can do so much better. You don't want to work for these guys. There'd be no culture fit, I don't know, they all have their own—"

"Culture fit?" Getu almost heard his mother's voice come back to him. *They'll never let you in*, she'd chided before. Getu said to Jeff Johnson, "I could be a guide, an interpreter between your world and my world."

"They already have guys like me as interpreters, so to speak." Jeff Johnson's sympathy only sharpened his authority.

Getu's mother's voice practically rang in Getu's ear. Ask him the difference between an interpreter and a thief, she would have said.

"I have other skills," Getu explained. "I'm a trained street sweeper. I'm good with directions. I'd make a top chauffer."

"Getu, I'm afraid you've somehow been misinformed," said Jeff Johnson, avoiding Getu's eyes.

"But didn't you say you had something for me? And what else could it be, all this talk of working together?"

"Did I say that? Yes, I guess I was just, not being literal," and Jeff Johnson furrowed his brow and started to walk quickly toward the gate. Getu walked sort of next to him, sort of behind him, trying to keep up.

"Oh, a joke," Getu laughed uncomfortably, walking quickly, trying to sound friendly, but wondering what to do next.

"No, it really wasn't, but I can see how you'd take what I said—" Jeff Johnson said, stopping.

Getu lifted his right hand out toward Jeff and said, "Well, I was just joking with you, too." Getu imagined his mother's voice again, this time aimed at him. *When someone slithers out of a tight spot by saying they're just joking, they're not just joking. Never let anyone get away with that. Never do it yourself.*

Jeff Johnson awkwardly approached Getu's outstretched hand,

and shook it quickly. "Still, I wish I could, Getu. I don't know how this happened. I really wish—"

"I really wish, too." Getu didn't know what else to say, watching this vague but powerful expectation unravel before him.

"Stay optimistic, Getu. Things will work out for you. I'm sure of it. For a guy like you," and Jeff Johnson had so much passion in his voice, so much hope and promise that Getu almost felt ashamed by the impossibility of his situation. "I'm sorry. I'm so sorry." He felt like he was saying this to himself, his mother, Mr. Jeff.

"For what?" Jeff Johnson said.

Getu didn't know why he suddenly felt so guilty, but he also felt he was meant to. "I'm sorry for everything," Getu replied, then added, "Thank you for everything."

"No, thank you for everything. I'm sorry for everything," Jeff Johnson responded.

Getu composed himself, pushed away thoughts of his mother, their house, the enchanted future on whose doorstep he had briefly lingered. Had he made a mistake, and if so, when, how? Or was his mother right, had he misplaced his trust, believed too much in these elusive words? He'd wanted to save their home, but he also wanted to be an exception, an exception to the rule that he'd seen proven over and over again that someone like him could be so easily swept aside, his home cast aside, his dreams cast aside. He wanted to prove his mother wrong, but more than that, he wanted to prove everyone wrong, the whole setup wrong, the whole system that marked him from birth and placed him at the mercy of the powerful, relative as that may be.

Getu thought about this as he walked Jeff Johnson around to the side exit and said a rushed goodbye, parting words—some combination of "Good luck" and "Take care"—back and forth a few times. A line of blue and white taxis circled the gate like a moat around the property; like so many, they, too, were not allowed to enter. Getu watched Jeff Johnson get into the first one, and as it sped away, the line inched forward. Getu waved until Jeff Johnson's taxi was out of sight, and Getu imagined it twisting down the road, down the dark hill, past the empty lots, the barren slope below. Getu pictured his house leveled, nothing left in the city but the huge spotlit structure looming beside him, its tinted bulbs attracting his gaze again, captivating his attention like gleaming jewels, and he wondered if somehow he could still collect on what had turned out to be an illusion of a promise. For wasn't a door still left a little ajar?

Getu adjusted his tie that hung loose around his neck, then walked up to the entrance of the Sheraton. A new set of guards was standing there.

"Can we help you?" one asked blocking his path, the other ignored him.

Getu didn't flinch. "I just stepped out for a minute," he said to the guards. Getu felt the thick stack of business cards in his pocket and pulled out the fourth from the top, carefully removed it, and handed it to the guard. "My name is Elias Isaacs with the WHO. I'm an interpreter here to meet a client." Getu spoke with ease, and he was ushered in, the tall glass doors flung open.

Mekonnen aka Mack
aka Huey Freakin' Newton

When my family moved from Ethiopia to the US, we bounced around a few places before ending up in Brooklyn. That was in 1989, the year Yusuf Hawkins, a Black child, was murdered in Bensonhurst by a mob of white boys, the year *Do the Right Thing* was released, and both riots—the one just a few neighborhoods away and the one on screen—gave me a sense that I had something to learn about race, real fast. I was eleven years old and got the warnings to keep clear of Howard Beach, where a young Trinidadian man had been attacked and killed by a group of white guys a few years before we moved to New York. And stay far away from Gravesend (the message is in the name, I heard), where Willie Turks was so battered on Avenue X that some judge called it a lynch mob in Brooklyn, but for the rope and tree.

In those days, I, their young, naïve son, was more of a resource about America to my parents than the other way around. I would pick up lessons through school or friendships or television while my parents worked jobs where they labored in back rooms or were otherwise invisibly kept out of the way. But none of us could teach each other about race in this country then.

In fact, it wasn't until they arrived in the US that my parents knew they were Black, and even then, they didn't know how to understand it. My parents thought in terms of tribes and ethnicities, regions and lineage. While filling out forms at the immigration office, my father pored over the options for color: red, yellow, white, Black (there was no box for "other" then, and had there been, he probably would have chosen it, and who knows what elaboration he'd have written on the dotted line). My mother looked at her yellow-hued skin and checked the box for yellow. My father checked red since in Ethiopia, that's what he was called—kay—the color that tinted his medium-brown skin. He marked me down as red, too. The immigration officer corrected the forms. Africans, he said, are Black. Lesson one.

From that day on, my mother believed in the possibility of two identities: we were Ethiopians, no doubt about it, and maybe we might become African Americans concurrently, but why worry about it, she said. My father declared that no, not African Americans, but Africans in America. My parents had grown up in a system with its own stratifications (light, brown, red, black along with Amhara, Tigray, Oromo, Kembata, and all the other eighty-one tribes that stacked up to form the social framework in Ethiopia). They carried that thinking over to the US. It did not translate; they could not let it go. I tried to cut through all that complexity and said, "Why aren't we just Black?" My father, who was privileged enough back home to get us here, retorted, "Mekonnen, you are not *just* anything." To that my mother agreed. And so ended the conversation—any real racial identity I developed would not be negotiated at home but was between me and the world outside.

Before I enrolled in school, I started to take note of a neighborhood clique of kids who called themselves the African American All-Stars. Word was the group formed in the 1960s by some liberal-thinking, power-embracing, mature-beyond-their-years middle schoolers who looked up to Malcolm and MLK and Fannie Lou and Lewis and Baker and Belafonte and all those who shone brightly in that revered constellation. Knowing no one in my neighborhood, I started to pay attention to this group who fashioned themselves as oral historians keeping old languages alive, and their messages seemed to hold some key to my new identity.

Every weekend, the All-Stars gathered in the back of the playground and did step dances passed down class by class, year by year. I didn't know where the choreography came from. Someone said they were old African dances taken up by enslaved men and women in the South and brought up North during the Great Migration. Whatever their origins, the moves were perfected over decades there in that playground. I wanted to join them as soon as I saw the boys making their bodies big, stretching their arms, stomping in great gestures, cupping their hands to their mouths and calling out, and the girls, pretty in the sunlight and show-stopping smiles, responding with writhing hips and dips and spins and their own calls. Then the dancers got quiet and just swayed to a poem by Maya Angelou. Someone read from Amiri Baraka, then Langston Hughes, "The Negro Speaks of Rivers," the last poem that ended every session. *I looked upon the Nile. . .* The girls snaked their arms, the guys moved like snake charmers coaxing their dance. The fellas fell to their knees (I thought, Lord, how could you not bow down to those girls?) *and raised the pyramids above it* . . . Boys on one side, girls challenging them on the other, and the boys submitted by stretching up their hands, and the girls let their fingertips touch the boys' fingertips. They spoke the next words into their huddle—a low, haunting murmur—then positioned themselves in one clear line. *Ancient, dusky rivers.* They stomped to the back of the playground, their backs to us onlookers. *My soul has grown deep like the rivers.* Applause.

And so before I joined the All-Stars, I had set out to make friends with them; I aspired. The All-Stars would gather on Saturday and Sunday mornings and dance and recite for anyone who would listen. I'd go out and watch as they performed in front of the walls at the back of the playground, where kids often played handball and graffiti artists painted huge murals of peace and love. We gathered together there and kept to ourselves in a neighborhood that also kept to itself in a city that seemed threatening to our innocence, and our bodies, too.

Anyone could try out to join the All-Stars, but membership was hard earned. They tested us hopefuls, calling out names and dates of the great and barely known Black historical figures, giving us books to study at the library, some written by former All-Stars, making sure we knew even the minor players in our past. I was grilled at every chance, no opportunity for my humiliation passed over. I got it worse than the others; to them, I had more to prove. I almost dropped out and told Kareem, the captain and alpha of the group, that I'd had enough, but he pulled me aside.

"You can't quit," he said. "You need this more than anyone. I never seen a Black person know so damn little about being Black," he told me.

"Why's your way the right way?" I asked, and he thought about my question for not even a second, then said, like he'd rehearsed the pitch, "We're offering a way to make it through. Right way, wrong way, it's a way through. The All-Stars are soldiers. This is your boot camp. You need this, kid," he said. "Bad."

I was sitting against the playground fence, and I remember the way his hand felt when he put it on my head, a paternal touch. He told me he'd coach me when I needed it and was true to his word on that. He pushed me; I pushed myself; I kept going, though it felt like hazing, and at times like plain harassment. Because who had to read twice as much as the rest? Who lied to his parents and took that old, red, graffitied, overcrowded 2/3 train into Manhattan to get those obscure books for the older kids (I could have probably ordered them from the branch down the street, like everyone else did, but they said I oughta go that extra mile), then carry a huge stack of books back down those big library steps, past the stone lions, through seedy Times Square, then on the 2/3 to Grand Army Plaza and down Eastern Parkway, turn left at the C-Town, and head on home? Who had to dance the longest, take the towels home to clean them (and clean them again if they weren't fresh enough)? Who had to go steal ice from the fruit carts outside the bodega to cool us off after practice? Who practiced longer, was asked the most questions, was measured against towering standards? Who at every turn seemed to be challenged, tested to see how bad was the desire? So at times it felt like pure, plain torture to within one inch of my life, and at other times, I felt like I was being taught survival skills so important that my very being depended on them.

The most important lesson was that the All-Stars lived by a single word, a guiding principle. Pride. When the rehearsals lagged, "Say it out," someone would shout. "Pride," we'd reply. I thought it was cheesy at first, but there was an urgency in those voices. "Say it out!" "Pride," a little louder. "Say it out!" "Pride!" We'd yell, and jump and pump our arms and work ourselves into a frenzy, then back to practice, back to the lessons, the language, the dance, the song.

This was my life on the weekends; during the week, I was in a tracked magnet program (a cruel caste system all its own) due in large part to my perfect test scores, my parents' friend letting us use a room in her home to gift us the right address to get into the right school, and some other magic mixture of luck and opportunity. I sat in the back of an all-white class, ate lunch with all-white friends, played sports on all-white teams, studied in the all-white library (even the books were by white writers, and none of the ones we studied on the weekends ever sat on those shelves). I transferred into the class late, and I learned later from those classmates that they had their own racial awakenings that year: they hadn't noticed they were in a white class till I got there. Just like that, I had established two distinct groups of friends: my school friends and the All-Stars, a sixth-grader juggling a highly compartmentalized life that matched the rhythms and patterns of segregation in '80s New York.

The New York summer, already brewing with its thick, mingled smells and heavy, wet heat, was dense on that late June day after I finished sixth grade. Kareem stood in the sun and led the announcements about who had made the cut. The new recruits waited around sweating from the high temperatures and the anticipation. The All-Stars chanted the names of each new member, and every inductee got a white T-shirt with "All-Stars" printed on it in red, yellow, and green. As the T-shirts were handed out, the initiates got up to accept them and joined the All-Stars standing in a huddle in the shade.

When there was just one shirt left and five of us waiting, Kareem said, "This last shirt goes out to the person who was born in the country where we got our colors." He pointed to the red, green, and yellow lettering on the shirt, the colors of the Ethiopian flag. I was in. It was a sweet victory, and the shirt was my trophy. I was even given a tag chosen for me by the older kids, what they'd call me, what I'd spray paint on subway platforms or abandoned cars: Huey Newton. On my T-shirt, in black marker: "Huey lives! Tough as nails!"

We wore loose T-shirts tucked into baggy jeans dyed red, green, or yellow that were held on our waists with big buckled black belts. We wore black high-top sneakers and bright white socks. We boys had high flat-tops and messages shaved into our fades. The girls gathered their hair into tight buns on the top of their heads and smoothed down the baby strands around their hairlines into swirls and patterns that were reshaped after practice with ubiquitous hair spray and cocoa butter. Head to toe, our style made us look bigger than we were, wider, taller (and our mothers didn't mind because we could grow into our clothes over time, and so they lasted us longer before we passed them down or consigned them).

We listened to hip-hop as it blasted from cars, from boom boxes, from turntables at block parties, and played it on a tape deck during breaks from practice. We liked De La Soul, Monie Love, MC Lyte, Run DMC, and LL Cool J. We loved Afrika Bambaataa, Eric B. & Rakim, Public Enemy, and Queen Latifah. We could do without the Beastie Boys, 2 Live Crew, and Jazzy Jeff and Fresh Prince (until "Summertime" came out, and we started looping their stuff).

None of this is to idealize; the All-Stars were no saints, none of us. Even Kareem, who had such nasty things to say about other races that I wondered how a twelve-year-old kid, even one as tall and boisterous as Kareem, could hold all that bitterness in his unformed body. And I'm convinced some of the older kids pushed around us younger ones because they finally found a way to exercise their power in a city that seemed to stomp it out at each turn. In fact, two or three dropped out and ended up in junior gangs that sprung up in our neighborhood with names spun off hip-hop groups (modeled after N.W.A. alone: N.W.T., Niggaz Wit Troubles; N.W.E., Niggaz Wit Enemies; N.W.S., Niggaz Wit Swagga).

The All-Stars were no saints, but they were a buoy. They didn't give me the puzzled looks that cut short conversations about race, like at home or in class. They didn't say things like "Just don't pay attention to that." Or "You're imagining things." The All-Stars always had an opinion, something for me to think over. And no matter where the conversation went, they always brought it back to pride. Pride the lesson, pride the method. Shame, too, when pride was lost.

Shame is a powerful lesson.

For most of my seventh-grade year, I had achieved what I thought was a balance of worlds, delicate maybe, but I was living it; that was my life, a golden moment I had hold of, and all was copacetic up until one Saturday afternoon on the way back from an All-Stars meeting at the public library on Eastern Parkway when Kareem and I put a rift between us that couldn't mend. We were all walking by the corner store by Grand Army, and I said the shop had the best array of candy on this side of the East River that I'd seen. Kareem told me he didn't ever step foot in that store. I asked why not. Kareem said, in a low-pitched voice, "Don't even get me started . . ." then he drew an imaginary boundary around the storefront, making it clear he wouldn't cross that line as he cursed under his breath, a minutes-long tirade that made me step back, ending with "These Koreans come here from Beijing or Shanghai or wherever, *no* passport and *no* papers, and they take over our blocks, my block? All of y'all are okay with this?"

Some of the girls laughed, but it was a dismissive kind of laughter that echoed as we gathered under the plaza arch where kids hung out in the cooling shade beneath the immortal, triumphant Union soldiers. Kareem got more defensive, folded his arms, cursing even louder at Korean store owners, at "the whole lot of them for their invasion of my part of town."

My silence was a provocation to him. "Back me up, Huey. Don't you know all Black folk in New York City take issue with this?" He looked at me and continued, "You never had problems with that store, with *them*."

"Never had problems, Kareem."

"Never? Not once ever? Bullshit," he cried out, and the girls giggled again—at him, we could tell—and he didn't like that. "I said bull*shit*," Kareem yelled, grabbed my shoulder, and I could see he was going to get something out of me one way or another. "They're fucking colonizers. Don't you know about colonizers out there in Africa? Things that wash up on the Coney Island shore: nasty hypodermic needles, oil from tanker spills, and little boatfuls of Koreans set to storm my block." He was yelling so loud that a group of neighborhood kids had gathered around us smelling a fight.

"That's not the Koreans," someone said. "That's Cubans and Haitians in the boats."

"This ain't no D-Day invasion, Kareem," someone else yelled. "How many boats you seen?"

Kareem went on with his ranting, and then to defuse the situation I said, "You know, *I* came to this shore, Kareem, in a way. Me and my family came to this shore, and you've got nothing against me."

"But you're not coming into my neighborhood taking something from *me*," Kareem said.

"Yeah he is," a girl yelled provocatively. "He's just like the rest of them, taking your spot, Kareem."

"Is that right, Newton?" Kareem said playfully, but as he looked me in my eyes—down at me because he was a good five inches taller—I could see the idea land somewhere in his mind, and he began to think it over, then he pushed his right shoulder against my right shoulder, hitting mine back like he was cocking for a fight. "Trying to rob me, huh? I see you, Newton." His expression got more serious, and he pushed my torso turning my body in circles, and the All-Stars gathered close and started calling at him to cut it out, but the other kids pumped for a fight. Kareem glared at me in a way that scared the shit out of me. I wondered what was happening to the friendship that we were forging with so much effort and kindness and time that it had transformed into a true filial bond because ten minutes before that I would have called him my brother, but right then, he didn't seem to know who I was.

He kept on, "Why you think you can hide some of your life away like that, live in two separate worlds like that, your Black world and your immigrant world? Or is it your Black world and your fancy school world? What're you hiding away from me? Let me in," Kareem's eyes brewed, some buried old upset surfacing.

Someone from back of the crowd yelled, "You can't let this skinny little wash-up kid lie to you like that, Kareem."

"He hiding something, they all is."

"Fight it outa him."

The All-Stars, on the other hand, were saying, "Stay calm, stay cool, boys. Keep your cool, boys," and things like that.

I said, "I took nothing from you, Kareem. I've got no beef with you. Let's just let this lay here and leave it be." My words were wavering, soft, and even if they had been hard and sharp, the intensity that showed in his eyes made me realize he wasn't open to what I had to say anymore. He heard me, but I couldn't sway him.

He rhythmically hit his shoulder against mine, spinning me around, and cars circled the plaza, and I was getting almost too dizzy to stand. Kareem didn't seem affected at all but kept on strong. "Those other worlds of yours are not your shield, hear? We been wasting our time on you, Newton? Motherfucker didn't learn a damn thing. That's plain as day, plain as that right there," he said, pointing up at the bright blue sky, and my gaze followed his lifting left hand so I wasn't ready for it. I felt my head jerk, the muscles in my neck relax when his right fist came at me. I staggered back and sought balance, and my hand went up to where my cheek pulsed. I tasted metal, I thought, then ran my tongue on my salty gums. The All-Stars lunged toward Kareem now, but the rest of the crowd was cheering us on, and Kareem was jumping up and down in place like he was skipping rope.

He could have kept going, I saw, but I also could tell then that his anger was taking on the form of a deep hurt, and we were both in so much pain. I put up my hands in surrender because I didn't want him to take all of what he had stored up out on me, and I didn't want to hurt him, either, and yes, fuck, I was hiding something, and he knew it, and he was hiding something from me, and I saw it, his agony right there in his eyes, his anguish, maybe even his hate. I had a secret that some would say I was willing to go to my grave with the way Kareem can fight, but Kareem won with one punch, and that hurt reflected back in his eyes, and the spoils of his victory: he got a story out of me, and he got my shame.

The crowd dispersed when the fight defused, and when it was

just me and the All-Stars, I said to Kareem, "Something happened to me," and he didn't gloat, didn't lift his arms like a prizefighter basking in glory, but just shook his head and sat on the ground to listen.

The All-Stars joined him, and I took my place in the center of the circle. I told them every detail I could think of. I started by saying my mom had given me a whole two dollars for lunch the day we had a school trip to the Cloisters (a couple of the All-Stars wanted to know what those were, and I told them it was like a huge castle you get to if you take the Manhattan A almost all the way to the end of the line). I bought a hot dog when we had our lunch in the park and ended up with a dollar left over, which I wanted to use for two candy bars on the way home.

I was in this store weighing the pros and cons of a Whatchama-callit against a Kit Kat when the proprietress tapped me on the shoulder. I thought she was going to ask if she could help me, but she asked me to join her outside and spoke quietly like she had a secret to tell me. She whispered that her husband was out of town that day, and she was busy. This meant, she was saying, that there was no one there to follow me around like usual. She asked me if I could just wait outside. She would buy me what I wanted and bring it out to me. I told her I had just wanted to browse that day, and I walked away.

The day after this, my magnet friends and I were on our way to the Botanical Gardens, and I still had my extra dollar in my jacket pocket. They wanted to stop off for a snack at that corner store that day. They always had extra lunch money and went there all the time when they were going to Eastern Parkway to visit the gardens or the Brooklyn Museum or the library. I walked nervously toward the store, and the proprietress saw me again, and she gently blocked me at the door. "My husband is gone," she whispered apologetically, pointing around her. She shrugged as if to say there was nothing she could do, and she seemed to believe it. "Next week, come in then." She asked me to wait outside again, just me, as my friends went in.

None of my classmates were bothered by this. I looked at my closest friend there, Tommy, who was my lab partner, and my study-buddy in homeroom. We were on all the same teams together, and he was by far my most trusted friend in the group. He didn't turn around, just passed over a boundary I wasn't allowed to. I didn't want to go home yet and I didn't want to stay. In fact, I couldn't work out what I felt. So I called Tommy's name from the door, and he turned. "Mack, what're you doing?" Tommy asked me. "The lady wanted me to wait out here today," I said repeating what she'd told me. He nodded as if to say she was an adult and we were kids, so she must be right.

I gave him a dollar and asked him to do the favor of buying me two candy bars. I remember his shaggy mop of feathery blond hair bouncing up and down as he crossed the threshold into the store. I stared inside from the window and watched him look at the new magazines, saw him considering the array of sodas, and watched as Tommy played with the others as they picked through the cheap toys that were stacked on the counter near the register. I stood at the window and waited.

When he was done shopping, Tommy handed me my candy bars, and that was that. Except that my magnet friends and I didn't talk about it afterward. Deliberately avoided the whole event, by which I mean what had happened that day at that store was pains-takingly avoided. I could just tell. They continued to frequent the store when they walked by, but I didn't go back much after that. Come to think of it, yeah, not at all. And those friends never asked why not but just changed the subject whenever I said I had to go home or wasn't up for it. That event hung in the air, and we sensed a wrong, but nothing came of that feeling, not even a word.

As I was relaying this story to the All-Stars, I could see from the looks on their faces—the disbelief, the gaping mouths, the wide eyes—that I had done something appalling. And something appalling had indeed been done to me. I felt like a kid who was the butt of a joke he didn't completely understand, smiling and laughing along to an insult I missed entirely.

Kareem didn't flinch, but the other All-Stars erupted.

"Come on now, think: what would Huey do?"

"We should throw you out!"

"What's the matter with you?"

"Use your head, Huey!"

"Have some pride!"

Kareem was the last to speak. "Bottom line, you paid her to treat you like a nigger. Shit, you didn't even pay her yourself—just had your so-called friend do it for you." He let his words hang in the air, then clapped his hands to summon the others to rise to their feet around us. He stood and the All-Stars lined up behind him. Kareem said to me, "Next time, Newton, this is what you do, watch." He clapped his hands above his head. "Like this: about-face," he cried, and they all turned one-eighty. Kareem let himself be led. He hollered, "Left foot goes," and the line lunged forward hard with their left feet, and the pavement shook. "Right foot goes," and the line lurched forward even harder with the right, and the pavement shook again. "Left goes," step, "right," step, "left," step, "right," step. "Pick it up, y'all! Left, right, light and tight. Now right, left, swift and deft."

After a full turn around the plaza, the line let itself dissolve and the All-Stars channeled the momentum of their march into an impromptu rehearsal, but Kareem came over to finish his sit-down with me. "You don't trust me yet or what? Why keep that from me?"

"It's just, I was trying to—"

"But see," Kareem interrupted, "what I'm asking is why you protecting your other world from me? What else you hiding about that other world of yours?"

"No, you don't get it, I protected myself," I said and started rubbing my jaw, which was still sore from the punch, and the long story didn't help. "I never talked about it with anyone, and then it got to be the kind of thing you don't talk about. To make it less real."

"Real is real," Kareem said. "Words don't make it so. Real is how this city is taking a knife to its own damn body, carving itself up and we're all left bleeding here because of it."

"What are you saying, Kareem?"

"I'm saying—we let you in, Newton. You in in, or what?"

"Yeah, Kareem, I'm in."

"We'll see, Newton. We'll see about you."

By 1991, the divisions in the city were shifting but still eroding the streets and wearing down trust, partitions around neighborhoods getting deeper like unbridgeable ravines. The Bensonhurst protests were raging. Someone even tried to kill Al Sharpton, but he survived. Then just before school started, the latest conflict in Brooklyn came to Crown Heights, where a Hasidic man ran over a seven-year-old boy and a seven-year-old girl, both Black. The boy died; the girl made it. That one especially resonated with me since they were kids, too. I guess it resonated in a different way with the Black men who then went on to kill a young Jewish man and the ones who killed an Italian guy who they said looked Jewish.

I was starting eighth grade and my life was changing quickly, too, when I became the new captain of the All-Stars. It was no consolation prize, though the open rumor was Kareem got together a faction to vote against me, and his ammunition had to do with that story, that fight we had, and what I deserved from the All-Stars, what I was committed to. I put in a lot of time before the vote proving myself, finding my own way to embody my place in the group, but the win wasn't total; nothing was right between me and Kareem again. Though he was already in high school by then, Kareem came to the small ceremony-of-sorts in my honor, but he stood in the back, didn't stay to say hello or congratulations, just lingered there as if it had to be seen with his very own eyes. He hardly looked at me, but I couldn't take my eyes off him, just stared at him waiting for a sign of approval.

I thought of Kareem a lot after that, wondering what it would take to make amends, and what would be there between us if we ever did. He never was on my mind more than the day in '92 when my father's best friend, Dawit Alemu, tragically died too young of a heart attack. The memorial was held out by Sunset Park, and I went with my father, who managed to get the day off. We had to take a bus ride that took so long the All-Stars joked I'd need a passport. My father had known Dawit all of his life, and they became particularly close when they both immigrated to the US, to Brooklyn. My father, a no-nonsense, soft-spoken, diligent, and proper man, took me to the florist with him to buy a simple bouquet, is what he said he wanted. When we walked into the store, the clerk, an old white guy, took one look at my father and started speaking immediately, "No, no, no!" He approached us shaking his finger. "We don't accept food stamps here," he said. The clerk walked up to my father and tried to usher him back out the store, almost pushing him out. My father pointed to his new shoes and suit and silk tie. "Do I look like I can't pay you?"

The clerk repeated, "No food stamps!" and my father looked to the clerk, then to me, then back to the clerk. My father must have considered walking out, and he must have considered taking all of his hurt out on the man with his fists (he had that same mix of pain and anger in his eyes that I'd once seen in Kareem's).

"Dad, let's go," I said, pulling on my father's jacket sleeve. "This isn't the only florist in town."

My father looked at me. "Stop it," he hissed. "This is the only flower shop I'm in right now."

The clerk said, "The problem is you Negros think your food stamps are as good as gold."

My father said, "We're Ethiopians."

This meant nothing to the man, so my father said, "I want the nicest flowers you have."

I pleaded, "Dad, let's get out of here. This man doesn't deserve your money," but the clerk stopped me from leaving and said to my father, "All right, all right. We have a lovely selection. Which ones you want?" and he paused and added "sir."

"I want the best," my dad said.

"Dad, this isn't it," I said and stepped between my father and this clerk. I kept motioning to my dad that I wanted to go, and all I could think was to leave. All I could think was: about-face. Left, right, light and tight. Right, left, swift and deft.

The clerk tried to assure me then, "It's okay, I thought you were one of them. Just hold on." He chose a big vase full of orchids and lilies, and brought it over to my father. I thought of the All-Stars, how we gathered together in the back of the playground in a city that feared and loathed and misjudged our bodies in ways fatal or brutal or cruelly banal. I thought about what the All-Stars taught me—what we taught each other—in moving our bodies so they embodied poetry, exuded the wisdom of those before us, lifting the weight we carried off each other's shoulders, turning our shared inheritance into art itself. With no tools and no instruments, using nothing more than what we came into this world with and what we fought this world to keep, to uplift, I felt my legs and arms pulsing. Right there in that shop, I could almost hear the songs we'd sing, the words we'd recite, feel the pavement vibrate under our collective steps. I felt the force of us all with me as I stepped forward, bent my body low, let my hands extend outward, and a leg jut out just so. I pulled the shopkeeper into my dance as he tripped over my foot, and those flowers showered down at my feet as I took a bow and imagined the All-Stars applauding in the back of the room where the afternoon sun beamed in, turning a spotlight on the scene. The man didn't even know what happened. My father saw it, and as the man rose to his feet, we quickly walked to the door, but I got in one last spin, and one final bow. On the walk home, my father had a hard time finding the right words but eventually said, "Where did you learn a thing like that? Mekonnen, we must do what we can to keep our pride here."

"Exactly," I said.

"Exactly," he said.

We looked at each other a few minutes more. He looked like he was working out a difficult problem, making an intricate calculation. His eyes were distant and his mouth pursed. I looked away feeling sorry for him, worried for him. He might have felt the same for me; I still don't know.

I wondered how much pain he had escaped by avoiding these harsh American lessons about race until he was older and maybe better able to distance himself from them, or on the other hand, how much more difficult was it for him to confront this context so late in life, when perhaps the insults were more shocking and unexpected, damaged all the more? Who was better off, the All-Stars or my father? And of course, I couldn't help but wonder, where did I stand? I look back on what I learned from the All-Stars often, especially these days, and it's nothing I can name simply, but doesn't it have something to do with survival, and community, and above all pride, and shame, and dignity, and resilience, and camaraderie, honesty, acceptance, holding your body up tall, and hitching yourself to a past, making legends of the big and small victories of that past, and letting that past move through you and move with you and move you so that it's you deciding for yourself what you're worth? I wonder what my father and Kareem would say to that now.

The Thief's Tale

He didn't think it was possible to get lost in America, especially not in the early aughts, not in a city like New York with all these named streets and these big arteries and huge landmarks—all the pins in this expanse. Yet he found himself in Prospect Park at dusk with no idea where he was or how to get back to his daughter's apartment. She would be so upset at him, wandering off alone without any money or a map or compass or knowledge of the language or culture or any other means to return home. Once again in this strange county, he felt old—not old and admired, like he did back in Ethiopia, not an elder to seek out for guidance, not a wise man who would draw in pilgrims from miles away for advice, not a sage of a family who would approve of marriages and other contracts—just plain old. He felt old and even rather helpless, a little pathetic, which was a new feeling, and one he didn't care for.

He sat down on a park bench, the lamplight flickering above. There was nothing much to see anyway; the nightfall dimmed the quiet scene much slower than it would in his more equatorial home. It was a chilly, early autumn evening, and there were no more joggers on the path, no more bikers getting home, no kids out playing. He sat alone in the darkness for he guessed an hour on an unpainted bench beneath a yellow streetlight, and then a man walked over and took a seat next to him. The stranger was dressed in jeans and sneakers and a bomber jacket. The old man wanted to speak to the stranger, ask how to find his way to the subway, from where he figured he could retrace his steps, take the green line five stops back. The old man motioned to the ground, pointing down at the green grass, then moved his flattened hand out and thrust it forward, trying to signal the underground train moving ahead. The stranger nodded a little and said, "You . . . no . . . talk?"

The old man spoke quickly explaining he could speak very well, but, as could be expected, the stranger didn't understand a word.

It didn't stop the stranger from asking the old man a question, but he could only make out the words "the" and "have."

"Have?" the old man repeated.

The stranger pointed at his wrist, and the old man shook his head remembering he took off his watch when he'd arrived a few days ago, and though he'd meant to put it back on after adjusting the time, there was so much to do when he landed, so much his daughter had wanted him to see: so much shopping, so many sights, so many buildings and elevators to scale.

Then the stranger asked another question and again, the old man could only make out the words "the" and "have" again.

"Have?" the old man repeated.

The stranger took out his wallet and pointed at the old man.

The old man shook his head. He'd left his wallet by his watch, full as it was of useless currency.

The stranger asked another question and again, the old man could only make out the words "the" and "give."

"Give?"

The stranger took out a knife and held up his own wallet.

The old man said, "give," and pointed at the stranger's wallet, then made the sign of a phone.

The stranger was confused at first—not least of all at the lack of fear in the old man—then seemed to take pity on him, another experience the old man was not used to, and didn't much like, but the stranger led him to a neglected pay phone under a humming light. The stranger found some change and waited as the old man dialed his daughter's number. She immediately started screaming on the other end, yelling at her father, stirring up another unwanted feeling that he was not accustomed to and could not name before she asked where he was. The old man didn't know but gave the phone to the stranger, who said something the old man couldn't understand, which he figured was directions.

As they waited for the old man's daughter to arrive, the stranger took out a deck of cards, and they started to build a house as the two spoke over each other, understanding nothing more than the music of untranslated, unfamiliar language. In his quick tense staccato, the stranger told the old man about how much he missed his own grandfather. On his end, in a slow and languid vibrato, the old man told the stranger about the last time he'd had a knife pulled on him, and how the old man had walked away with that poor knife wielder's ear—literally—and his car, and daughter's dowry.

The house of cards between them fell, and the stranger started a new story about how he gambled too much and got himself lost all the time now that his wife left him. The old man, meanwhile, told a story about the last time he himself held a man up with just menacing threats as weapons, and how, in this way, he was able to secure a new apartment, a beautiful little studio that the old man's estranged mistress still, he assumed, enjoys very much to this day.

Their house of cards folded over, and the old man confessed that he'd trade all the treasure in the world to begin over again, and the stranger confessed that he'd trade all the treasure in the world to begin over again. Their house of cards collapsed once more, and the stories restarted about longing and trickery and twists of fortune. The stranger gestured like he was searching with a flashlight, which the old man took for swordplay. The old man moved his arm like an asp recoiling, which the stranger mistook for an ebbing tide.

When the old man's daughter drove up in her Volvo and frantically rushed to her father, she immediately started shouting again, and the old man was glad that the stranger couldn't understand. The old man silently nodded at the stranger before slinking toward her, and she embraced him, lovingly. His daughter gave the stranger a twenty-dollar bill for his help, but the stranger politely refused. The daughter tried to insist, but the old man stopped her, so she simply thanked the stranger as she got into the car.

The stranger tipped his hat at the old man, then walked off beyond the yellow glow of the streetlight and into the darkness. The old man was about to tell his daughter a passing thought, but the sound of the engine cut him off.

He began again, and explained, "Sometimes one gets lost in the dark, but if you have some tricks up your sleeve, you can end up the better for it," by which he meant he'd witnessed the small miracle of good timing, and also, without knowing the same language, managed to turn the tables such that, despite his empty pockets, he scored a bit of money from an armed robber with nothing more than a modest sleight of hand. He marveled at the vitality of this feat, but his daughter was already rushing toward the parkway rattling off a list of groceries she'd forgotten to get on her last trip to the store.

Kind Stranger

Addis Ababa was hardly recognizable, a city casting itself into a new mold: taller, more modern, more planned and plotted. I'd gotten used to crossing construction sites with big boulders and chiseled stone but nonetheless lost my footing and stumbled forward. Looking down, I saw a reclining man reaching for me. His head leaned toward his legs, his hands outstretched and clasping. He looked familiar, though it was unlikely that I actually knew him—I lived in the States now, and rarely made it back. It was hard to see him clearly in the long afternoon shadow of the cathedral. I knelt beside him to make sure he was okay.

"Are you hurt?" I asked, and tried to lift his head. I thought about calling for help, but he started talking without any introduction.

"Listen, my child." His voice was barely a whisper so I had to bend down. "One night near the end of the rainy season, I got caught in a storm. There was water—"

His voice cracked, so I reached into my shoulder bag to offer him some water, but he shook off the gesture and kept talking.

"I found myself jumping over the flooded gutters as I ran from the minibus toward home with my jacket over my head to keep myself a little drier, but you know how it is with the rainy season—a losing battle. The whole bus ride, I had to fight for space next to a boy and his damp, smelly goat; that boy showed no respect for his elders standing next to me like that. I was tired, and there was the boy and his soggy little beast, and the rain, and outside there were rows of yellow Mercedes, which I always thought I'd look quite good driving."

I was surprised by this deluge of narrative coming from a stranger, and then tried to do what I thought I should: I felt his forehead, which wasn't hot. I checked his pulse, which didn't race. I rolled up my sleeves and sat down beside him. I tried telling him to take it easy, but he had more to say.

"So that night was—how do they say it in the movies?—a dark and stormy night," he went on in English, adjusting his language for his audience.

"A dark and stormy night," I repeated. "That's what they say."

"Besides the rain, the power outage made it hard to see except for the bursts of lightning that lit up the street, lit up the homes, lit the acacia trees on the hillside. The lightning flashed just as I was about to take out my keys and open the gate, and that's when I saw her: Marta Kebede standing under a big black umbrella, looking the same as the day she was arrested back in 1980. I hadn't heard of her or seen her since, though I'd thought of her often, of course."

He said "of course" like I knew him well, like none of this should come as a surprise to me, and on top of that, the way he leaned his head close and whispered into my ear felt intimate, as did the soft way he grasped my hand. The only thing I could think of worse than unrequited intimacy was mistaken intimacy.

"Sir, I think you have me confused with someone else," I told the man. "Just rest. I think you're hurt. Let me get you a car. I could give you some money." When he declined, I looked again for a wound or sign of injury, but found none.

He didn't seem moved by my concern and just said, "If you have a minute . . . I just need to rest a minute. If you have a minute, I will take that."

I didn't really have time to spare. This was a short visit to see relatives, and almost every moment was accounted for. Yet out of obligation, I felt like I should probably stay with him just a little longer.

He didn't wait for my response and simply continued his story: "So I'd just seen Marta, the first time in decades, and there she was, caught in the middle of a storm. The lightning stopped for a moment and I could no longer see her silhouette. I tried to speak into the darkness, but thunder smothered my hello. I jogged toward where she had stood, moving with both excitement and hesitation, for the sight of her made me feel conflicting emotions: elation, dread, and also grief. Isn't that the way it is with grief, though? First we mourn the grief we bear, and then later we mourn the grief we've caused."

As he said these words, the helplessness on his face that I'd taken for kindness seemed to vanish. I thought that this switch was strange—that his emotions could change so easily, so suddenly and completely.

"So that night on that dark street, I called out again to Marta, saying the only words I could think of: 'Let's go for dinner.' It was an awkward thing to say, but once I had said something, I started saying everything. 'It's me, Gedeyon. Don't you remember? We were students in the same class at university—you were getting your degree in pharmacology, and I was studying chemistry. I asked you out on a date the first week, and you said no, and you made fun of my shoes, saying that they were farmer shoes, and that you wouldn't date a boy with farmer shoes because your father would kick you out of the house and your mother would drag you to the priest and drown you in holy water. I saved up a whole half year to buy new shoes, really nice ones, and I asked you out again, and you didn't know who I was. I told you I was going to be a professor and you said you wouldn't go out with me, but this time you didn't bother with a reason. I guess I must have loved you. How else could I explain the lengths I went to get your attention, your approval? I wish it hadn't happened that way, and I still wonder if we would have turned out differently if things happened some other way.' Isn't that a lot to say into the darkness?" Now he gripped my arm and lifted himself onto the boulder to sit upright.

"Yes, it is a lot to say." In any light, I thought.

"If she had acknowledged me, if things had gone a little differently between us, maybe I wouldn't have accused her. Did you ever live here during the Derg?" he asked, not giving me much time to consider what he'd just revealed. "I think you didn't. I think you lived somewhere Western, some wealthy country with peace and freedom."

"I know the Derg," I replied. "I was a child of the Derg, born of that era."

Gedeyon shook his head. "Those of you who left here when you were young or when the Derg was young, without more than a scratch, and had the luxury of living somewhere else don't know what some of us carry. You know what the Derg technically is, but you don't truly know. You know the Derg as a definition, a Cold War regime that lasted too long and did too much harm. But those of us who got to truly know the Derg over all those years, who knew it as an uninvited guest dropping in on each meal and in every interaction, well . . ."

I felt my face flush, and now it was the grip of guilt that kept me there as he went on.

"I had been tortured by the Derg—that's how I got to know it. Some of the students avoided school back then to reduce the risk of being arrested and just stayed home. But I went to school every day, whether there was a demonstration or the threat of arrest or nothing at all because we got free lunch at the university, and if I didn't go, I didn't eat all day. It was a simple fact of life. So I went to school every day and was arrested, and who knows why back then. Maybe I had a friend or associate who was suspicious, or maybe my hair was too long or too short, or my fingernails were too clean or too dirty. Maybe it was on account of my nice new shoes—who knows? But when the Derg interrogated me, lashing my feet, asking me to name names to get myself free, I gave them Marta's name. She was wealthy, had power, and I thought she could escape, that she'd have a better chance of surviving it than I would. And it's not that I hated her, but she'd stung me. Marta had stung me. Those subtle stings to pride—they're worse than the big ego blows because they're not like some obvious pebble you can remove from your shoe. They are like shards that you know are there but can't find and can't get rid of. Oh, Marta, I wish she'd never made fun of my shoes."

"So did Marta accept your dinner invitation during the thunderstorm?" I asked, trying to keep him awake since I was concerned at the exaggerated way his eyelids were beginning to droop.

"Well, I kept asking her to dinner, but she didn't say anything. I stood there waiting for another bolt of lightning, and when it came, I saw her far down the street talking to someone, but I didn't know who. The dark, the rain—everything was obscured. I approached her cautiously, ducking behind a tree, waiting for the right moment when I could finally go up to her and try to speak again. After another strike of lightning, she was alone at the mini-bus stop where I'd just come from. I walked over and stood next to her tall, illuminated figure. I just stared, hoping she would recognize me and start up a conversation. She eventually turned toward me, even smiled, and said, 'Good evening.' She offered to share her umbrella, so I shifted closer to her. But she didn't seem to know who I was."

"You said you last saw her in 1980? That's a long time ago," I said.

"Not long enough to forget a friend." The way Gedeyon twisted his lips with spite made me think this was a man of impossible expectations. "She should have remembered," he said. "The thing is, she has always been on my mind. I wrapped all this guilt up around Marta, all this significance and longing; so much so that I could recognize her anywhere, even in the middle of a blackout with just a flash of lighting to reveal her face. It never occurred to me that her feelings wouldn't mirror mine, at least a little."

"So what did you do then?" I asked, hoping he'd just wished her luck and walked away, but I already knew him well enough to be certain that he hadn't. And I couldn't walk away myself because his story now had a hold on me.

He continued: "I responded to Marta, 'Good evening to you as well,' and added, 'Don't I know you?' I thought that maybe she just hadn't given me a proper look yet, but when she turned and really examined me up and down with that judgment-filled face, she said, 'No, I do not believe we have met.'

"We began to talk. I didn't say much, just listened. She said she was going to stop by church to give thanks for how life had turned around for her. I realized this was my opportunity to ask about her life—maybe she would have a flash of recollection then. She told me some general details. She said there was a time she'd been in prison during the Derg, but that was then. I told her I had been thrown in prison, too, by mistake, and she said, 'What a shame.' She leaned a little closer to me, so I got the courage to ask why she'd been arrested, and she deflected, saying, 'Oh, I don't remember, and besides, does it even matter?' 'Of course it matters,' I said. 'Oh, I don't know,' she replied. 'They'd target you for the most absurd things.' She shrugged as if she didn't want to give it much thought. I imagined exactly what they must have said to her anyway. They'd accused her of being a bourgeois princess, more interested in the state of her closet than the very state in which she lived, skipping rallies to do her hair and dodging speeches to read fashion magazines. That's what they might have said to her because that's what I'd told them. That she was a nonbeliever, a threat to the cause. Those were the words I'd used to trade her freedom for my own. It had to be done."

I didn't know what to say to that.

"I'm sure you'd rather not be here." He stared at me with despair. "You left and avoided these difficult truths. You haven't had to see the heavy weight some of us carry around. Do you think I'm ashamed of having survived the way I did? Why should I be?"

I didn't defend myself from his misplaced accusation, which was softened by his fading voice.

"I never said I'm a good man," he went on. "I was just a regular man, but the Derg, it made me . . . it made me and it unmade me. It heightened my worst instincts. It gave me permission to be worse than I was ever meant to be or would have been in another place, another time. It gave my sins a platform, gave them cover, gave them cause. And for whatever reason I still can't explain, I took the Derg up on this opportunity to abandon my good senses and do as I pleased. I believe—really believe—there was good in me once. I guess I don't know that for sure, but I think it's true. I think I was decent once. I could have been a regular kind of man. Maybe I didn't have the courage to be better, or didn't have the luxury to be better. I couldn't avoid the hard choices. I was here, made here, unmade here."

He clasped my hand and held it closer, and the warmth of his breath on my skin began to repulse me. Why did I feel like I owed this stranger something? He seemed frail, and despite his bitterness, he needed me. I felt his forehead again, which was a bit hot. He put his cheek to my hand, pursing his dry lips.

"So the rain was just pouring down now, and the cars were whizzing by loudly, and Marta was almost shouting, telling me she'd not only survived the experience of prison, but that it also made her more self-reliant and tough. As awful as prison was, she had to invent ways to endure what she thought would be unbearable, what she thought would break her. She said she struggled but eventually created a space to be calm within herself. Gradually she was able to create a space to let joy enter her life as well, even there in prison—they were the most fleeting moments, but they were something. She found a way to make those fleeting moments last. She found a way to forget, which was the hardest accomplishment of her life. And when she learned how to do that, she found a way toward purpose. She hadn't cared about school before because she hadn't cared about much, she said. But she made a choice to get educated, and she was able to do it. The Derg loved to throw intellectuals in jail—the students, the professors, the writers—and the prisons during the Derg were the best schools in the country, as some say. Marta also met her husband there, and when they were both out—released or escaped or otherwise got free—they fled together to America, swept up in that wave of refugees, and landed safely on a shore called New England where they went back to school and started a family. She got a good job and didn't look back on that time except to acknowledge that she was lucky in the end."

Gedeyon stopped to catch his breath, and I said, "Well that's about as good an outcome as you could hope for."

"You could say that." He pressed his head to my hand once more. I could feel his fever now. He told me that he'd forgiven himself for the wrongs of the Derg, and damn anyone who judged him for that. "Damn you, too, if you're judging," he said. But he hadn't found a way to forgive himself for his other sins, and I saw then that he was making me his confessor.

"Is there someone I can take you to talk to?" I asked him.

"Would you rather me tell this to a friend? A friend who I want to respect and remember me well? Or tell my priest, who I have known all my life and who I respect? My family, who will carry forth my name? My colleagues in whose esteem I hope to remain? Would you rather me call it out from the rooftops and confess to the city? . . . Or should I tell a stranger visiting from halfway across the world who looks like she doesn't make the return trip all that often? And who has managed to be a child of the Derg without carrying the same load, but who should shoulder it as well?"

And he paused, and I saw the evidence I'd been searching for all along, an empty bottle of pills falling from his pocket, and I couldn't tell if these had been to help him or if they were what made him sick. I couldn't even tell if he'd taken them.

When I asked him, he just said, "Listen, child, to my last words."

What could I do but hear him out and share the burden of his secret now? I knew if I said nothing, he'd continue, and he did.

"I asked Marta, 'What was it like, being a refugee?' 'It's not for the faint of heart,' she said, sweeping her short curly hair off her face with her left hand. The strands caught the light and shined, and I thought I'd never seen her look so sophisticated, so strong, so completely out of reach. I was drawn to her, so I pulled in a little closer to listen.

"She told me, 'Not even my mother knew where I'd gone when I fled Ethiopia, not at first, but eventually I was able to send a letter, and then we corresponded as much as we could. When my family finally saw me after thirty-five years, they told me how good I looked for someone who'd come back from the dead.'

"I was gazing at Marta, clenching my fist so tight I felt my fingernails bending back, so I put my hands in my pockets and looked at the beams coming off the car headlights, circling her like she was encased in jewels, her body haloed by the glow of the streetlight behind her. She is still something, I thought. Not just someone who has reclaimed what's lost, but someone somehow ennobled by loss. I don't know how to explain this, but I looked at her like she was either my proudest creation or my most wretched punishment. I don't exactly know what I felt, but with false pride I told Marta about my own life, the basics: I was a chemistry and math professor, had a wife once, but it didn't last long. No children, my family mostly gone. I lived freely. Mine was what I called a content and unencumbered existence with routines, stability, and modest comforts, which was more than I'd been born with, and so I felt successful, for what was success if not to die with more than what you had coming into the world?

"Marta said I must be proud of all I was able to accomplish despite my time in prison. She added, 'Sometimes, things even out in the end. Karma, justice, and all of that.' 'Like an equation,' I replied. 'That we're always balancing.'

"She said something I couldn't hear over the rain, so I stepped a little closer, and when she craned her head to see if the minibus was on its way, I fixated again on the light glistening off her hair. I reached out to her by instinct. A car sped by and honked and I pulled myself back, which sent her umbrella out into the darkness, as if a strong gust of wind had caught it. Marta lost her step. She slipped on the muddy curb and fell onto the street, her ankle stuck in the gutter.

"She reached out, and I leaned toward her. She needed me—for once. So I reached for her, my hand nearly touching hers, and Marta whispered, 'Kind stranger.'

"And I froze, because even now, especially now, the Marta of my dreams and nightmares and fantasies, haunting Marta who had scolded me for wearing those old shoes, who had failed to recognize my achievement getting the new pair, who had talked to me for half an hour that very night and still had no idea who I was, now called me a stranger.

"I realized then, as she held her hand out to me, that she hadn't even introduced herself that night, hadn't told me her name, nor asked for mine. I was a stranger and always would be to her. I was frozen and the cars honked their horns, unable to stop, the beams of the headlights closing in, overtaking her, and she lunged desperately for my hand, almost a helping hand, almost a friend.

"When the ambulance came, there was really nothing left to do. I knew I could say with some degree of honesty that it had been an accident—a horn, the umbrella, Marta stumbling, me somehow not being able to get to her in time. I try to make sense of that moment. After all these years, I was given a chance to settle the past, but this wasn't the way, was it?"

He was posing a question, but not to me, whose name he'd never asked, a stranger who was there for him in his moment of need, something he didn't seem to recognize.

"Tell me what you think of my story," he said, and I didn't speak, didn't move as he leaned forward and rubbed the dirt off his shoes, caring for them like they were his salvation.

Medallion

Of course he assumed his cousin would pick him up from the airport, but because Nunu was caught up at the office, Yohannes was to take a taxi instead. Along with the keys, Nunu had left sixty-five dollars in an envelope under her welcome mat, which sounded like a small fortune to Yohannes. That is, until Yohannes asked a cabbie in line to quote the cost of his trip. The driver didn't say, exactly, but something like forty dollars, so Yohannes offered ten dollars less than this, which made the driver laugh. "First day in these United States?" he asked Yohannes, who nodded. The driver pointed to the meter on the dash, already at a dollar, and said, slowly and loudly, "We count going up here, not down."

On the drive, they wove through traffic on elevated stretches of highway that made it impossible for Yohannes to get a sense of whether L.A. was as chic as he'd imagined from the movies, whether America was as sparkling and welcoming as he'd been sure it must be. Yohannes anxiously watched the meter tick higher and higher, nickels, dimes, quarters, dollars, ten, fifteen, up and up as the cab seemed to move in place, the same view out the window of lanes of cars and a vague haze hanging in the air. After a long silence, the driver introduced himself, Bobby B. from Barbados. Yohannes introduced himself, Yohannes Bekele from Ethiopia.

"Nelson Mandela was here, what, four, five, six years back when he was released from prison around 1990, right," Bobby said, easing into conversation, holding the wheel with his left hand, resting his right hand on the emergency brake, like he was more comfortable driving stick.

Yohannes began, "Mandela is from South Africa, which is pretty far—"

But Bobby kept on, "Was it Mandela who said that for him as a kid, Hollywood was the stuff of dreams, and that his dreams are going to come true? His sure have, right? Are you here to chase a dream?" Bobby asked.

"I am here for school," Yohannes said.

"Then, little brother, you are definitely a man with dreams."

"Maybe," Yohannes said as they passed more palm trees peeking up from the highway overpass.

"What do you want from America?" Bobby asked.

"My degree," Yohannes responded. "That's what I want from America."

"A degree is just a single piece of paper," Bobby said. "You gotta want more than just a single piece of paper." Bobby looked at Yohannes in the rearview mirror with his eyebrows raised, expectantly. He continued, "A degree doesn't shift things much. What's one degree colder or one degree warmer? What's one degree south or one degree north? What's one degree more or one degree less? Eh, it's not much."

"Well, in terms of climate and navigational direction, it actually depends—"

"Not much at all," Bobby persisted. "I guess the only real question is, do you want wealth or fame?"

"I guess I've never thought about those," Yohannes responded, his desires seeming so modest in comparison. To be able to pursue an education and study and drink water from the tap were things he looked forward to, slight shifts in degree, perhaps, but to Yohannes, they felt like a whole new course.

"Well, you're young. Start to think about it. But don't wait too long," Bobby warned, turning up the radio, humming along, and tapping the steering wheel while Yohannes found himself tapping his toes, too. "Listen to these lyrics," Bobby said, then he sang the chorus about wanting to be rich, for a little love, peace, and happiness. "In America, people sing out their desires clearly. It's the only way to make them come true," Bobby shouted over the music.

That seemed reasonable, Yohannes thought, and Bobby pressed on, "What's your line of work?" Bobby asked.

"Engineering," Yohannes said. He'd done his first year of his bachelor's in physics back home and would finish up here.

"That's a good line of work, because it might, might, get you rich, and as a Black man in this country, that could just be the difference between ending up like Rodney and ending up like OJ as far as I can tell, you know, if there's any hope at all?"

Yohannes did not know, but he very much wanted to know, so he asked, "Could you kindly elaborate on your significant thoughts?"

"Yes. Yes, I can. See, you take it from me, you should get yourself rich and you should work for yourself," Bobby said, turning down the volume on the radio now that it was his turn to answer some questions. "Like me, I got no boss, I got no wife, I got no one to answer to but me. I may not be rich, but I'm no-hassle. Rich also makes you no-hassle. Working for yourself makes you no-hassle. As a Black man, I don't recommend working for anyone in America but your own self," Bobby said, and Yohannes was about to ask if everyone in this country was always fending for himself, taking taxis, making it from point A to point B all alone, but Bobby had more to say. "I mean absolutely the worst is the fact that you can find yourself running in place here very easily. Working and working and getting nowhere. You think you're making your way up, but you are not. Do you know what I'm saying?"

"Yes, yes I do," Yohannes confirmed, watching the scene outside also repeat again: palms, billboards, dusty medians, gas stations, rest stops, and he already could feel that sensation of speeding ahead and getting nowhere at all.

"You know what a token is?"

Yohannes shook his head no.

"You gotta learn that word. Memorize it. Token."

"Token?" Yohannes asked, watching Bobby's approving eyes in the rearview mirror.

"Token, yes. A token is no sign of wealth. It's something you pay the bus fare with; a token is a thing that tells you you're about to be taken for a ride! It is what they call tender, a kind of money, but of extremely limited value, and only good in certain contexts. A trinket! A fake coin. A piece in a game. You think you have this nice job, but no one takes you seriously. Even so, when the banquet lunches happen and the presentations and the ceremonies, there you are right there on stage, as if you are a chief officer. They'll take your picture, and you'll find yourself on the cover of all their brochures.

"So it's like a celebrity," Yohannes said, and Bobby squinted into the rearview, looking right at Yohannes.

"Um, not quite," Bobby mused. "Umm, it's not like that at all." Yohannes looked out the window waiting for Bobby to continue, and it was as if they'd rewound the trip and started all over, passing identical tall and slouched palms, same cars, same billboards.

Bobby asked, "Would you believe me if I told you I was once an exec, an executive, a junior partner at one of our fine city establishments?" Yohannes looked Bobby over. He wore a short-sleeve, button-down denim shirt, board shorts, a hat that said "L.A. Lakers," no watch, no tie, no blazer, nothing that would indicate "executive" of any kind. But who knew what executives were like in L.A., and Yohannes—wanting to please the first person he'd met in the city and not knowing the answer anyway—said, "Yes, of course I believe it. I could see you doing anything you chose; this is America."

"Oh, shit, you are screwed, little brother," Bobby said, putting his right hand on the back of the passenger's seat and twisting to look at Yohannes directly for a second before refocusing on the road. "Shit, you are seriously screwed." He paused as if taking in the weight of what Yohannes had said before continuing. "But it's true, I was a bank executive, but my job was fuzzy and didn't make much sense, because my real job, unbeknownst to me, was to be a token. That's why I was getting the big bucks, not as big as the bucks that everyone else in my suite was getting, but big bucks nonetheless. But anyway my boss, a white dude, had portrayed himself as a real do-gooder. Divestment, Oxfam, all that. He was trying to get on some board of some big philanthropy. He had this office full of African and Caribbean trinkets—souvenir cloths, teeny clay pots, cheap masks, all kinds of junk. He had a huge poster of two smiling Black kids so big it could have fit on the side of a bus. Next to that, a framed pixelated blue poster of Nelson Mandela that looked like it had been printed on a dot-matrix that was running out of ink. Every time I stepped into the office, I felt like I was walking into a tourist-trap gift shop back home, airport adjacent. You know what I mean?"

Yohannes did know exactly what he meant.

"At some point, when someone wears too much cologne, you have to wonder what he is trying to cover up. That's what my grandma says, 'Too much cologne, a big stink to hide.' So if you used your eyes, you'd think, this guy's crazy about Black folk! But listen closely and you'd hear the story he was trying to hide. He would always say things that he shouldn't have been saying, and I was his get-out-of-jail-free pass. That was my job. When he said something offensive and rude in front of a client, he'd turn to me with, 'You don't mind that I said that, do you, Bobby?' I would stand there like a deer in headlights, and just like that, he's off the hook. I imagined that in my absence, he would say things like, 'Some people might find what I'm about to say offensive, but my employee wouldn't mind, so it's okay. He's one of them.' So guess what I did?"

"What did you do?" Yohannes asked, only able to see Bobby's mouth in the rearview mirror now that his chin was lifted, and the way it pursed up at the edges with mischief, Yohannes thought this guy seemed so wound up, nothing Bobby said next—no matter how outlandish—would have come as a surprise.

"I gave my two weeks' notice is what I did," Bobby said in a very serious voice. Except for that, Yohannes thought; that came as a surprise. Bobby's eyes were serious, too, his chin tucking into his neck, both hands on the steering wheel at ten o'clock and two. Bobby continued, "I took my savings, bought this cab, bought a medallion, which let me go into business for myself. I mean, my own hours, no one to answer to, and fuck if this isn't one of the only ways a Black man can drive around this town without

Medallion

worrying about getting pulled over. A no-hassle life, little brother, is your goal. Here, young brother, is my card," Bobby said, holding the card up over his right shoulder as they pulled up to Yohannes's stop. The concrete highway gave way to a concrete stretch of road and a concrete apartment building with a concrete pathway leading to a concrete fence in front of concrete patio furniture. Bobby parked and the meter was at forty-eight dollars. He entered some numbers in a log and said, "Take my card. Call me if you need some help with a job while you study."

"Work is complicated. You need certain papers and—"

"Say no more, I know about things like papers, but how much does school cost? Even if you have a scholarship—do you?"

"Yes."

"Full?" Bobby twisted in his seat and looked right at Yohannes.

"Full."

"Well, I'll be, little brother. Congratulations. But does that cover board, books, printing, transportation, pens, notepads, folders, and the nice-to-haves?"

"I . . . isn't there a library?"

"What're you supposed to live on, eat with, brush your teeth with . . . ? I mean, damn, a little brother needs a little extra, am I right? I could help you get some pocket money while you settle in. Done it a thousand times for a thousand guys just like you. Just like us. You could drive some hours in this cab, and it'll make all the difference in the world. I promise, I'll be good to you."

"I'm not sure," Yohannes said, feeling uneasy not just about Bobby's proposition but about his whole new life here in the US, which would apparently lack not only the nice-to-haves, which he knew he'd happily sacrifice, but also the must-haves.

"Look, this is a great gig here. In the desert, you wanna be the guy selling water. On the beach, you wanna be the guy selling sunscreen. And in L.A., you wanna be the guy selling rides. This is the most in-demand job here, you'll see."

"But I don't really have the time or even—"

"I just want to help out a brother, young brother. At least, this ride's on me, okay? Don't worry about it. Welcome to America. Welcome to your first and last, one and only free lunch."

"Lunch?" Yohannes asked.

"Free thing," Bobby clarified. "Now, go get rich," he said.

* * *

Yohannes hadn't had a good look at Bobby's cab the first time around, but now that he was about to be driving it, he took in every last detail. Bobby's cab was yellow with purple and white checkers painted on a racing stripe from the trunk up to the hood ornament, a faux-gold light bulb. The seats were upholstered in purple velour, the mats had images of the pyramids, and the seat pockets were full of magazines for passengers with an array of address labels, none of them for Bobby: *National Geographic* from Hal's Auto, *Vogue* from Center City Dermatology, *Sports Illustrated* from L.A. Smiles, DDS.

This was his new office, Yohannes realized, and he was grateful. He'd called Bobby up after a semester. His hours had been cut at his campus job, and what he'd been able to afford was quickly becoming out of reach. At the start of the new year, his rent rose, the cost of food increased, gas, bills, everything getting higher and higher.

"I told you we count going up here, little brother," Bobby said when Yohannes called and told him about his predicament. "You just need a tow to get you from where you are to where you need to be," Bobby assured him, "and I'm the one to do it."

Bobby hadn't been the first person he turned to. He tried his cousin Nunu, who was often out or trapped at the office or staying over at her boyfriend's place. But it wasn't like Nunu had the money to lend, or good enough credit to cosign a loan. She didn't have the answers, either. The one conversation they had about his finances was bleak.

"Sorry, cuz," was all Nunu could think to say. "Maybe this is not the year to be a foreigner here, without means."

"What year would be better then?"

"Good point," Nunu yelled out like he'd answered his own question, and Yohannes didn't understand why.

"What am I supposed to do?" Yohannes wanted to know.

Nunu said, "You know I can't float you."

"Don't worry, I'll keep looking."

"Be as persistent as you were to get here in the first place," Nunu advised. "There's really no other option."

That's when Yohannes realized that he might have to go back home, and even then, he wasn't sure how he'd cover the airfare. While his parents had given their savings to get him to the States, it was only enough for the one-way ticket. It hadn't occurred to anyone to buy the return fare. Yohannes explained this all to Bobby, who eased his mind. "There's no such thing as being stranded in America. Here, the way out is up, up, up."

Bobby clapped Yohannes on the back, then clapped his hands and rubbed his palms together. "Now, before I go handing you the keys to this here kingdom," Bobby told Yohannes, "I need to be sure you're orientated. Are you ready for your orientation?" Bobby asked, leading Yohannes up to the cab. "Pay attention, you will be tested."

Bobby handed Yohannes a book of maps of the city, which he was told he'd need to memorize. "No problem," Yohannes said.

The town seemed like it had been custom made for cars, and all the streets had names and signs and all the highways had numbered exits and all the roads had lights and lanes, even ones only for turning left or right or going straight—so much simpler to navigate than the unmarked roads he knew back home.

The streets had a clear logic to them, but the cab was messy and jumbled, and Yohannes worried about the wisdom of accepting Bobby's offer. But if he were to make a map of where he was now, he would see only this one path. It's not that he didn't like Bobby, he liked him fine. He would have gladly become his acquaintance, maybe eventually a friend. But Bobby had a certain charm, a certain charisma that already was pulling him in, and Yohannes came here with his own desires. He was starting to sense that Bobby had plans for Yohannes, and there was nothing more dangerous than being cast as an understudy in someone else's dream, Yohannes was starting to learn.

"Okay, your new life awaits. Orientation starts now. Take notes," Bobby said, and Yohannes readied his pen, leaning in to listen as crowds moved up and down Sunset Boulevard. "A cab, it is your office," Bobby said and opened up the door to show Yohannes all the paperwork he had tucked into the glove compartment. "A cab, it is your library," he said pointing to the books lined up at the foot of the passenger's side. "A cab is your all-weather, all-terrain transportation," Bobby said, kicking the wheel twice. "It is your love chalet," he said, popping up his eyebrows, opening up the armrest to reveal a half-melted candle, matches, and a box of condoms. "It is your bed away from home," he said and pulled a blanket out from under the passenger's seat. "It's even your sideline side hustle if you want one," he said and opened the trunk, took two lawn chairs out, and set them up. Bobby took out a board that said "SALE" and placed it by the back bumper. The trunk was full of cassettes, videos, bongs, packs of incense, colorful ashtrays, books, random items of clothing, random items of all sorts. Bobby explained, "Lost and Found."

"Really, people just abandoned all this stuff?" Yohannes asked, motioning at a car phone, a set of weights, a set of silver, a set of five identical alarm clocks.

"Sure these were all, quote, 'lost and found.' You know, left behind, released, parted with, let go of, all the same," Bobby said. He invited Yohannes to take a seat with him and said, "Got any other questions?"

Yohannes sat down next to Bobby as men and women walked up to the trunk of the cab and flipped through Bobby's rummage sale. "Yes, I have a question," Yohannes said. "How much will it cost me to rent this cab from you and how much money will I make?"

"A stickler," Bobby said, sounding annoyed. "It's cool, it's good that you want to know that. And you know what? It depends entirely on you," Bobby said, leaning back in the lawn chair and opening a soda.

"It depends somewhat on you, as well," Yohannes said.

"It'll fall into place over time. Let's start with the big picture for now. First, work harder."

"I work hard, always—"

"You have to listen carefully, little brother. Here you can't just work hard, you have to work hard-er. Harder than the boss, harder than the boss's nephew, harder than the kid that reminds the boss of himself when he was that age. You have to work harder than everyone else because, I'm sorry to tell you, you will be tested and you will be doubted and you will be classified before you open your mouth. Once you open your mouth, it'll be 'Is that English?' and 'What did you say?' or 'I can't understand your accent,' or 'Speak clear,' or 'If you can't learn English right, go back home,' or 'If you don't like our language, then why'd you even come here in the first place? We didn't invite you.'"

A woman wearing a flowy strapless dress and big floppy hat atop a loose red afro walked up to the cab, waving her finger at Bobby. "I got ya," she said. "Where on earth have you been?"

"Sweetheart, I've been where I always am. Here for you," Bobby answered, winking her way.

"You owe me," she said, shaking her head, her floppy hat bobbing with each whip of her neck from one side to the other.

"You're the one who stole my heart," he said, "so don't you owe me?"

"Oh, enough talk from you." The woman looked at Yohannes. "You with him?" she asked, pointing at Bobby with her thumb.

Yohannes nodded.

"Get yourself unstuck from this guy," she warned. "Get yourself out of his way. He says all the right things, but damn if he's not going to leave you hanging in the end."

"Sugar," Bobby whispered. "Take it easy. Here, have a cassette," he said. "Let's see, I got Sade, a lovely lady for a lovely lady." He flipped through the stack, then pulled out two more. "Digable Planets because you are out of this world, girl. And Al Green because you know why."

She took a step back and crossed her arms over her chest, her floppy hat falling over her left eye.

Bobby kept pleading, "I'm a gonna call you today and we'll work it out then, okay, sweetheart? Don't fear, Bobby always comes through."

"No, he don't," she said.

"He will," Bobby replied.

"He better," she said.

"My word," Bobby responded before she walked off looking like she was not at all convinced but also like she had a hundred other places to be.

"Aw, she didn't look back at us. Too bad," Bobby said. "If she had, it'd have meant that she still liked me, don't you think? So what was I saying? Oh right, work harder. I start each day listening to my power anthem, 'I Wanna Be Like Mike.' You know Michael Jordan?" Bobby asked.

"What did she want?" Yohannes asked, not yet ready to yield.

"Who? Susan? Oh, it's nothing. It's an old lover's quarrel kind of thing. Private between a man and a woman, you know?"

"Not exactly. Do you owe her something?"

"You know, she feels jilted, and I borrowed some things from her—little things like anyone in a couple might—and she wants them back. I'm not trying to do wrong by her. I just haven't gotten to it, you know?"

"I guess," Yohannes said slowly.

"You ever had a girl?"

"No," Yohannes admitted.

"Oh, okay, little brother. Then you don't really know what I mean. Just take my word for it—some women, it just pays to stay away from, to be honest. And Susan is one of those keep-away women."

"That just doesn't sound right to me, though, Bobby. It seems like if you just give her back what you took—"

"That's the past. We are here to look ahead. So back to Michael Jordan."

It was clear that Bobby wasn't going to give him the answers he wanted yet. He'd ask about Susan later. Yohannes focused back in. "Michael, you said? You mean Jackson?"

"Jordan, Jordan. Michael Jordan. Where'd you say you was from again?"

"Ethiopia, it's in East—"

"I know where Ethiopia is. Haile Selassie and shit. What do you watch out there, track and field? Michael Jordan is the greatest man our country has ever seen. Don't get me wrong, I'm a Magic fan too. You like Magic?"

"Sure, but no one should mess around with magic."

"Agree, Magic is powerful, but Mike can triumph over Magic any day."

"I have to look him up."

"Yeah ya do. How does a person not know who Michael Jordan is? Tall dude, quick, literally flies through the air. Flies through all the blocks and obstacles. Soars around and around and above and beyond everyone. Nothing touches Mike. He is who you want to be. He is who we want to be. Are you writing this down?"

Yohannes started writing, "Michael Jordan, idol, pilot."

"I sing that 'Wanna Be Like Mike' song all the time." As if to prove it, Bobby sang a few bars, and a couple walking by stopped and joined in, twirling, "I wanna be, I wanna be like Mike."

"There ya go," Bobby said, waving at them. "I've got that song and all kinds of music right here," he yelled to the pair, pointing at his open trunk, but the couple walked off, twirling again. "So I sing that tune every a.m. I touch my medallion, pat down my afro, you know? I eat a breakfast of champions: eggs, avocado, and coffee."

"Avocado?"

"Avocado," Bobby said, making a circle with his fingers. "Round, green skin, big seed in the middle, fleshy."

"Ah, we call those mangos," Yohannes said.

"What are we gonna do with you, Ethiopia? Avocado is avocado, mango mango, okay? Avocados are green inside, mangos are orange. Why aren't you writing this down?"

Yohannes wrote, "Avocado is likely an unripe mango."

"You know what the real goal is?" Bobby asked as leaned back even farther in the lawn chair. "The real-real goal is to get your own medallion. It's like a permit, but it costs. Once you have that you can buy your own cab and work any hours you want. You don't have to take bullshit from anyone. Not from me, from no one. That is freedom. That is no-hassle. You can drive on the side while you take classes, while you save up for a house, save up for your freedom."

"How do I get a medallion?" Bobby seemed to be the sort who was hard to deny. Susan's warning to get unstuck from this guy came back to him; he was worried that he'd walked into a trap. Yohannes came to the US to expand his opportunities, not to be tied to a liability. Yohannes wondered how quickly and neatly he could extricate himself from Bobby.

"Your options are limited because of your situation, but I know a guy who can make your dreams come true," Bobby said. "It'll cost you sixty K on sale, inclusive."

"What's that translate to in American dollars?" Yohannes asked.

"Sixty K translates to sixty K. Sixty thousand US dollars."

"No way, no way can I get that. No way," Yohannes said, and he stood and started to back away from Bobby.

"All right, calm down, stay put. I can still help you out. I know this other guy who, well, he can fix you up with a temporary one, but just don't ask too many questions, okay? He doesn't like that."

"How much are those?"

"Already with the questions."

"But I have to know because—"

"It's okay in this case. Those are just five K, which translates into five thousand USD. It's nothing, five K, a sprint, a little fun run, nothing like a marathon. I know it takes time to save, but you work for me for a few months and keep your expenses down to practically nothing, you'll get that easy in no time. I drive nine to five, so you can take the cab out some other off hours and we go from there."

"I can't work weekday mornings," Yohannes said, taking hold of the spare car key, calculating that five K could be more than the assets of a whole village back home, but all in all, it was less than what it would cost him to get home and come back. Maybe this was his way to hold on here just a little longer. So he gave Bobby his passport as a security deposit, as was their arrangement, the only thing of value he had.

"I knew you'd say yes," Bobby said taking out a box from a hidden compartment in his trunk, flipping through a stack of cards, handing over a fake license to Yohannes, informing him that his name would be John Smithers, and he was a resident of California, though all the rest was true: height, five feet, eleven inches; eye color, brown; photo wasn't him but looked like him, same chestnut skin, wide forehead, dark cropped hair.

"This might not be your American dream," Bobby said, taking hold of Yohannes's shoulders, "but this is your stepping-stone dream. Your starter dream. Your starter American dream. You'll earn enough money for your expenses, sure. But also save up for that medallion, then get yourself a cushion, get established, do the things that you need to do to put down roots: finish your education, and if you choose to stay eventually, have a business, a home of your own and some spending money, which, if you want to tie yourself down like some men do, can do a lot. You can live the whole damn American dream script, if you so choose. You can have a wife, a white picket fence, two kids if you want 'em, a dog or a cat or a parakeet or whatever, a minivan, the whole happily ever after. This isn't a half plan, like get a scholarship and come to university in the US with no idea of what this country is at all—no network here, no helpful connections, no offense. I have a real plan with real long-term potential."

Yohannes didn't know if he should agree, but he didn't entirely disagree either, for a new desire was taking root in his mind, in his heart, the one thing and one thing alone that would make this all work now: Yohannes needed to get his medallion.

* * *

Yohannes's schedule was tight. Up by 4:30 a.m., study until class, class till 1:00 p.m., work, an early dinner, pick up whatever shift he could get from Bobby. He'd change into a suit and tie because he found he got higher tips, which he'd also get by not wearing a hat or sunglasses, and smiling excessively, too. He always let the passengers choose the music, how much the windows were or were not rolled down, the route they preferred, and, if they wanted, a mint or a piece of gum. He experimented with what seemed to please the customers the most, streamlined his systems, and came up with a style that had him bringing in more than Bobby right away. Bobby took a cut, of course, then Yohannes got a cut for his expenses, and Bobby put the bulk into an interest-earning account so he could get to that medallion as fast as possible.

When his parents wrote to ask how things were going, Yohannes would write back about how much he was learning living in L.A., and he meant it. When Nunu asked, "How are you settling in?" during one of her brief, intermittent check-ins, Yohannes could say, "It will all come together," and meant that, too.

That's why it surprised Yohannes when he kept falling behind, no matter what he did to catch back up again. He was behind on paying fees for one thing after another. Bobby was right, nothing was free. On top of that, he learned that his next semester offer would be renewed at three-quarters rather than a full scholarship. And so bit by bit, he came to rely on Bobby more and more.

When he cut back his course hours in the spring semester to pick up more shifts, he had no problem dodging Nunu at first, but she started to press him on his half answers about school and homework and his plans and friends. He practiced the slippery art of evasion, learned from Bobby over the months. He told Nunu that L.A. really was like in the movies, magical and full of possibility.

"Cuz, what movie are you talking about? I mean, where are you hanging around and who are you hanging around anyway because . . ."

"There's Bobby. He takes me all around town."

"But you really gotta watch out for—"

"He looks out for me—"

"Because L.A. is full of dreamers and schemers, and you don't want to end up on the receiving end of a dream or a scheme because—"

"We have a good time, and he's helping me out—"

"There's a certain type here that you just can't—"

"We explore the city from east to west to up to down—"

"A certain sort of charmer here that can really take you for a ride."

"I'm no token," Yohannes said, mimicking one of Bobby's slogans, but she wouldn't let up. "One day, I'll introduce you to Bobby," he promised, knowing she'd be hard to pin down, too.

One semester turned into two, and he'd been picking up all of Bobby's off-shifts for over a year. Yohannes had almost saved enough for his quarter share of the scholarship when his school revoked the offer altogether. It would be impossible to pay for school on his own, he thought, so maybe he should just focus on the medallion instead, since he was so close. That way, eventually, he could cover the cost of any education he wanted outright.

Bobby supported this goal fully, praising Yohannes for earning so much, creating methods to optimize his time and cash flow. Yohannes was learning the city better, knew exactly what times of day to go to Venice Beach and Hollywood and Brentwood, studied the university calendars, figuring out when parents would show up to spoil their children or when the frats and sororities would host their most lavish parties, and when alumni would flock back, and how they all loved hearing that Yohannes, too, wanted to go to college someday. He kept current about awards season, not that any celebrities ever rode with him—they had limos and such—but the outer rings of their entourages might need a cab. He was up on sports, not because he liked them, but to figure out which rivalries would attract the big crowds and where to be on game day. Bobby was impressed, seeing Yohannes earn exponentially more than him every time. "Maybe I should give you a job running my business," Bobby joked once. "How can I possibly let you go?"

Yohannes said, "Good student, good teacher."

* * *

Bobby had always been a relatively reliable kind of guy toward Yohannes. Passably so. He wasn't always on time, and he sometimes came up short on cash when they went out for a bite, but that was just Bobby. Bobby was Bobby. Yohannes allowed Bobby a bit of give when it came to the details since Bobby always came through in the end. But when Yohannes was about ready to buy his medallion, Bobby kept forgetting things. He forgot the number of his contact who could get him the medallion, forgot his contact's address, forgot his contact's last name, forgot his contact was going on vacation for a week, forgot his contact would be on a spiritual retreat for a few more days, forgot his contact had moved to a new apartment. One day, Bobby forgot to drive the cab over for Yohannes to pick up his shift at all. Yohannes called to check in and though Bobby apologized, he forgot to drive the cab over the next day, too, and the one after that.

When Yohannes went to track Bobby down, he realized he didn't know where Bobby lived. Didn't know much about him at all. Bobby's card had his phone number on it, and nothing else. Bobby was not returning messages.

Yohannes hoped, somehow, their paths would cross when fate had determined the moment was right. But to help fate along, Yohannes went to the major cab stands. He took the bus, looked out the window in case he might just stumble upon Bobby pulling up in his painted taxi one day. He went back to the airport, knowing it was a favorite spot for Bobby, and that is where Yohannes found him, waiting for a fare.

Yohannes opened the cab door and took a seat in the back. He knew that cab so well, and sitting in it again made him feel like he'd come full circle, ending just where he'd started, once again a passenger with Bobby at the wheel, watching the reel rewind, the scene reset for take two.

"Where to?" Bobby asked without needing to look up.

"Land of dreams," Yohannes said.

Bobby smiled back in the rearview. "Little brother, I've been meaning to catch you. Let's get you scheduled, let's get things back on track," Bobby said. "You got an important pickup soon—that medallion of yours."

"I'm counting on you for—" Yohannes started.

"It's coming. It's going to come through. Just you wait and see," Bobby said.

"When, though?"

"Don't you trust me?"

Before he'd come to the US, there was only a very limited, very particular number of things Yohannes trusted, very little he put his faith in: his family, his church, the land he was raised on, his ability to solve an equation, his willingness to outwork anyone he'd met. Since arriving, he had no choice, really, but to trust others without knowing more about them than their first names, sometimes. "Do I trust you?" Yohannes asked sincerely. "I guess that's the life I'm leading now. I put my trust in you, and I have to hope you don't let me down."

"I will not let you down, little brother. Bobby B. always comes through."

"I guess I have to believe that, and I guess you know it."

"Chin up, little brother. You know," Bobby said slowly, like he wasn't even listening to himself anymore, hypnotized by the repetition of cement medians, the palm trees, the billboards, "what you have is a ride in the express lane, brother," Bobby reassured. "You'll be all set up in record time, little brother. Record time. You'll be all set up faster than you can say 'American dream.'"

"American dream," Yohannes said, forcing a smile. "There, I said it."

"That's it, keep saying it out loud. You gotta say your desires out loud here to make them come true. American dream. A medallion. A medallion is your dream, your freedom, remember. Work for yourself, invest in yourself. An investment in you. That is the number one American commodity, everyone invests in themselves. That is how we do it here. And to invest in yourself is to invest in your future. If I knew any other way to get to the American dream, I might recommend it, but this road is the only road leading anywhere for guys like us coming from where we're from looking the way we do if we don't want to wait around forever for our lives to change. From now on, it's all green lights ahead."

"American dream," Yohannes said.

"Declare your intentions, little brother. Yes, manifest, manifest."

Yohannes looked at the man behind the wheel who seemed in charge not only of the direction of this taxi, but of his whole future, and Yohannes wondered if there was any choice but surrender. He had come here for an education, but this was not what Yohannes had in mind. These were not the lessons he expected, but he could see now he had a lot left to learn. He figured, how bad could it be to keep working with Bobby a little longer? Maybe, he'd get a reliable cab, maybe buy a light bulb hood ornament of his own like Bobby had, maybe paint his cab green like a fresh start, still working toward that promised life, waiting for it to begin.

Sinkholes

A typical high school classroom in the middle of Florida in the mid-1970s. And when I say classroom, what I mean is not so much a room, really, but more an annex? In the back of the main building? Picture a tiny trailer hitched to a semi. We are the overflow, and we make do. Ms. Verne stands in front with an eraser-mark on her sleeve, her glasses at the tip of her nose, frizzy blond-gray hair radiating from her falling braid.

We have just read *Invisible Man* by Ralph Ellison, and Ms. Verne says we're going to do a class exercise, which we follow up with the usual groans and hands thrown in the air. Ms. Verne stays cheerful, assuring us that this is a good one. She says Ralph Ellison wrote about race and asks us to think about what we know about race by coming up to the board and writing down a slur.

English isn't my first language, but it's been ages since I found myself truly unable to grasp a lesson or a class discussion. But when Ms. Verne starts us off like that, I think I must have misunderstood. Everyone seems to feel that way, though, and there is a long, tense minute when the class says nothing, does nothing, waiting to gauge what kind of permission or pressure this is, exactly. Josh, class prez, shoo-in for homecoming king even as an underclassman, gets up first and boldly writes *cracker*. We are stunned, but the silence is filled quickly by the click of high heels when Jenny, his on-off girlfriend, yearbook deputy-editor, brunette-blowout writes, *kike*. Our shock is audible. Grungy, tough, brilliant Sara writes in such tiny letters that no one can read it. "Wooly-haired, okay. That's what it says, okay," she tells us, reluctantly. Pete, pitcher, pinch hitter, assistant coach, nearly every other position as the only one any good at baseball in our small town, goes up to the board like he's stepping up to home plate, lifts his perfect arm like an ever-coiled spring and writes *spic* then *chink*. "To be thorough," he boasts like he hit it out of the park. Someone claps twice; the pace picks up.

Right about now I notice glances darting back at me as I sit in my usual spot in the last row. Here I don't stand out as the poorest kid in the class, as those relegated to the annex are pretty abject, but I am suddenly all the more aware of my status as the only Black kid in class, the only person of color at all, member of the only minority family in this "traffic stop" town (by which I mean a little pass-through stretch of road that dips down to twenty-five mph for a handful of miles and gets most of its revenue from speeding tickets handed out to drivers racing between two major cities). I realize *they* are all waiting for *me* to write *it*. The collective focus shifts from Ellison, the teacher, and the chalkboard to that word and me, simultaneously the one person permitted to speak it and the one who, maybe more than most, doesn't dare.

So I wait, and I avoid their furtive little peeks over at me and stay put as the chalkboard quickly fills up with every slur that a few dozen high school kids can think of. Eventually that granite starts to get overwhelmed with made-up slights, too (has anyone ever heard of curly-toed or flirty-breathed or buxom-bearded, I mean . . .). I don't even think it's intentional that the very middle of the board seems to be reserved, and slowly all these words circle this space like a drain, written sideways, slanting, shifting from the perimeter of this emptiness like the very arms of the Milky Way around a black hole. I watch the space in the center stay blank as the rest of the board gets whiter and whiter. I am bewildered, confused, and simply decide to deflect expectations as I contemplate what I am witnessing.

Well, actually this shit happens all the time in Florida, sinkholes open up out of nowhere, and they suck in everything around them. They can swallow up a room, easy. They can even take in a house, car, the neighbor's pool. There's a famous one at the edge of town that grew almost a quarter-mile wide, and it became a nature preserve where people pay five dollars to stand right against the edge and try to see inside, wondering what might appear: a city, a universe, memories, some vision, not to mention a reminder that this swampy ground is shaky ground and count your blessings.

I've never seen a sinkhole like this, but that's exactly what it is, right up there on the board, and we are teetering on its edge. Ms. Verne stares at me with a helplessness I've never seen in an authority figure before. I am waiting for this moment to pass.

So, a little about me: I like chess. I play a bit with my friends, and I've read a few manuals and have watched some of the games by the grandmasters. I even followed what Bobby Fischer was up to when he got in that standoff with Karpov a few years back. As I sit still and Ms. Verne is still, the two of us just glaring each other down, I start to think this looks a lot like a standard stalemate situation: the point when the person who's up has no legal move to make, a draw is called, the match is abandoned, the board cleared, and the whole thing resets. But Ms. Verne won't let this end in a draw, and I can't call the draw, and you see, that's the thing about a sinkhole: once it starts to suck you in, there's really no good way out again.

Ms. Verne, she keeps asking for volunteers, and out of a desire to please or just to fill the horrific silence that hangs in the hot damp air, and the horrific silence that has made itself known in the middle of the board, volunteers do indeed keep going up. She encourages them, but keeps looking at me, pushing her stray hairs back. I look at her, then the board, then her, at my book, at my hands, at my wrists, wondering if I can see my pulse, which is racing from anger and disbelief now. I do the thing you do when you don't want to get called on, which is pretend you have something much more important to think about and can't be bothered, and rather than write anything up on that board, I write a note in the margin of my book, "This is happening."

"Anyone else?" she asks, voice soft now that we all are very aware of what a clusterfuck she's led us to, and I imagine she is even more aware than we are. Josh gets up again, and we all perk up with uneasy curiosity as he approaches the board, presses the chalk to the center, stops, then, as if he's changed his mind, moves his hand up to a small bit of space at the very top by the metal frame that maybe only he can comfortably reach. *Raghead*, he writes. Jenny, on-off girlfriend, goes up next and just at the edge by the lower frame, she quickly writes *Jarhead*. "It's not really a racist slur," Jenny explains. Then, very clearly and very slowly and with her mouth moving as wide as it can to express that extra emphasis, Ms. Verne says, "Thank you, Jenny. So much." While she speaks, Ms. Verne has got her eyes on me again. In fact, all eyes are on me. Me, I'm not playing dumb and I'm not playing vicious, but I'm also not playing along. I stare right back at Ms. Verne, and I can't help it. I really, honestly can't help it when I smile just a little at the corner of my mouth, lopsided, but there it is.

And right then, she knows for sure and I know for sure that it's going to be up to her to get us out of this, and so she says (To whom, me? To the class? To herself?), "You can't let a word have this much power. This word is not powerful unless we make it so."

Which of course makes me think of the awesome power of this word. This word is in fact so powerful that we are all speaking it that moment, even though we are not saying it. This gets me thinking about all the times and ways this word is said without being articulated. And how often do my classmates think this word in my midst, looking right at me, thinking the unspeakable, and how would I know? As Ms. Verne wipes literal drops of sweat off her brow, I study the way my classmates look as they share this one suppressed and pressing thought, and they don't appear to be any different. They don't seem any nastier, don't look any scarier. They look like they always look. It all seems so practiced and so easy for them to be thinking what I know they are thinking, looking cool, cold, and staying silent. Chilling to see that it's impossible to read this word on their faces. You'd think it would raise a brow or turn down a lip, but no, everyone looked same as ever as they focused on these unarticulated letters.

I imagine walking up to the board, to that dark silence in the middle, and I swear I can almost foresee the afternoon I'm kicking Billie's ass in Trivial Pursuit and he yells it out as a synonym for "jungle," and how a sense of power lights his eyes before he says, "Dude, oh sorry." I can almost foresee driving past the cops lining our little expanse of road as my friends laughed and hollered for me to be careful because this highway was a "you know what trap" and I better slow down to five under or end up six under. How easy it was to foretell getting stopped by the cops several times a month at least, hearing that word as I put my hands on the wheel and avoided their eyes. Or I can nearly predict the heartbreak overhearing my first love, Elisabeth Elroy, stumble over her words when she's telling Randall Jones the joke, "What do you call a, um, a— Black person who's, you know, shi—you know, on the toilet for nine months?" I can even almost foresee the entanglement of anxiety I feel at junior prom when the headmaster's drunk daughter can't look me in the eyes when she says, "I wish you'd get expelled, the way you make me fear what's in my head." That would come later, but something was revealed to me there in the blankness on that board.

I decide to speak, finally. Something has to shift and even if I can't dig us out of this hole, well, maybe I can stop the sinking. When I raise my hand, my teacher looks like she's about to fall to her knees and praise the Lord that I have finally joined in, but rather than walking up to the board, I just ask her, "You say don't give this word power, but doesn't this prove its power? Isn't that what we've just demonstrated here, in some empirical kind of way?"

Ms. Verne says, "It's not more powerful than us, than we let it be."

And I say, "There is gravity at work here, ma'am, can't you feel that?" I am pointing at that blank space on the board that is dragging us in. "How do we respond to that?"

And Ms. Verne says, "It. Is. Simply. A. Word." I hear a gasp or two as she walks up to the board, takes the chalk from the trough, and pauses, breathes like she's shoring up courage or maybe thinking through the consequences of what she's about to do. I am stunned to see her follow through. Fast, hastily, Ms. Verne writes in really big letters that fill that void, with the whole class looking at her, then at me, and then at her, and then down at the floor.

But the thing is, as soon as she writes it, she takes the eraser and wipes its every last trace, first circling the middle over, then letting that radius expand, clearing the expanse of granite, the chalk falling away as she moves the eraser farther and farther out.

The Case of the
Missing ████████████

Day 100: . . . and Still no Verifiable Sign

One hundred days! One hundred days and we are no closer to finding the absentee ███████████ than we were yesterday, last week, last month, the beginning of this ████. We've been waiting for answers, truth, and yet all we know is ██████. And as far as we can tell, none of our esteemed colleagues in the diaspora media are having any luck with this story, either, though we all are counting the days, watching them add up to █████████████. A tip of the hat to the journalists and writers who started tracking this ████ first. Hat tip to the ones who have been keeping us informed from the start, best as they can given the complete ██████████████████, trying their hardest to make sense of this somehow. Tip of the hat to the readers who continue to follow the ███████████, patiently bearing with us as we muddle through.

Dear readers, fellow writers, fellow citizens of the world, it's already getting late in the season, the year 2036 will soon come to a close, and we feel like this has been going on for years and decades, and may go on for years and decades more. There is no end in ████. Along these lines, we regret to report that the letter we published a few days ago was discovered to be a ██████, and so the fate of the missing ████████████ remains unknown. We are so sorry to disappoint. We are at a ████. Frankly, this would be a comedy if it wasn't ████, a tragedy if it wasn't so ██████. We need—we demand—transparency, we need accountability, we need answers, truth, leadership.

Day 80: Mayday, Mayday, SOS

We're told it's a sinking feeling when you're strapped into the seat of a moving vessel and there's no one steering anymore. Who's to say a ship—any ship, of leisure or of state—won't careen right off the deep end, so to speak? At times like this, one sends out a signal, sends out the distress call. At times like this, it's protocol to call all ports, alerting them the captain is AWOL, has left his post, send a "Mayday, Mayday, save our ship."

Repeat: the captain is AWOL, there's no one at the helm. Calling all ports, calling all stations, calling on all nations: Mayday, Mayday, SAVE OUR SHIP.

Day 58: At Sea, Closing the Case?

We are nearing the ████████ mark, and finally, we at *The Exile Gazeta* have come upon what is truly a promising ████ (we write about this to ask for your help in proving/disproving) that the ████████████ has been heard from in the form of a letter to the national newspaper. Is this letter real? We are putting all of our humble resources toward this tricky task of authentication. The letter states simply:

"My people: Do not fear, it is I. Do not take down my photos, but do feel free to erect statues."

It appears the letter was sent, believe it or not, from a barge on the ▮▮▮▮ Ocean, and if this is a legitimate document, well that would be farther than our limited assets would allow us to investigate, for we've not the funds to pursue a high-seas caper to a fuller resolution than this.

Why is he on a barge, if he is on a barge? ▮▮▮▮▮▮▮▮▮▮
▮▮▮▮▮▮▮▮▮▮▮▮▮▮▮▮▮▮▮▮▮▮▮▮▮▮▮▮
▮▮▮▮ That is regrettable news, if it's true. And if it were true, ▮▮▮▮▮▮▮▮▮▮▮▮▮▮▮▮▮▮▮▮▮▮▮▮▮▮▮▮▮▮
▮▮▮▮▮▮▮▮▮▮▮▮▮▮▮▮▮▮▮▮▮▮▮▮ take charge of things. Instead there's ▮▮▮▮. Alas, we ourselves have tried to do our part, but we've just been chasing over three thousand dead-end ▮▮▮▮ that have taken us literally around the world (our phone logs prove we've placed calls to countries from ▮▮▮▮ to ▮▮▮▮).

This chase has had us all at the edge of our seats for ▮▮▮▮▮
▮▮▮▮▮▮▮▮▮▮▮▮▮ to be honest, while some of us are sad and blue about ▮▮▮▮▮▮▮▮▮▮▮▮▮▮▮▮▮ our beloved country of origin, mostly we're just hoping for better days ahead. We're hoping ▮▮▮▮▮▮▮▮▮▮▮▮▮▮▮▮▮▮▮▮▮▮▮▮▮▮▮▮▮▮▮
▮▮▮▮▮▮▮

Thanks to all who offer ▮▮▮. It's been a long, long road, and we hope this story has finally come to an end.

Day 56: #WheresOur███

Social media mavens have created the hashtag #WheresOur███ to share theories, rumors, and gossip about the mysterious fate of our absent ██████████. Our favorites so far include:

> @GoodGovernanceNow ████████ is not a whim. ████████ is not a hobby. ████████ has literally mocked us . . . #WheresOur███

> @AfricansForObama Couldn't take the pressure so jetted off for a dose of retail therapy in Dubai #WheresOur███

> @LumumbaIsInTheBuilding @AfricansForObama If I see him when I'm there, I'm demanding a refund #I got receipts #WheresOur███

@SearchingUnderEveryRock posted a tweet storm of speculations:

> Hush, ███ listening. ███ watching, ███ still watching . . . #WheresOur███

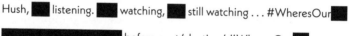

> ██████████ before next 'election.' #WheresOur███

> Mumbai financing Bollywood musicals #CantTakeItWithYouWhenYouGo #WheresOur███

> Silicon Valley begging Facebook to give up our data #WheresOur███

> Turned into a ███ #WheresOur███

> Hiding in a ███████ daze #WheresOur███

> Turned into a ██████ #WeGetTheLastLaugh #WheresOur███

> Turned into a ████████ #WheresOur███

> Turned into a ████████ WheresOur███

> Turned into a █████████ #WhatGoesAroundComesAround #WheresOur███

The tweet from @GlassHalfBull echoed a common refrain: "Post Arab-Spring commemorations, is autocracy simply shutting down? #WheresOur█." In the Twitterverse, a few suggested the twenty-five-year anniversary of the Jasmine Revolution that brought down entrenched autocracies—in Libya, in Egypt—had something to do with this. They wonder if authoritarianism is finally out, evaporating into a ██████████, and only democracy will do from now on. Who knows if the world is moving in that direction or if a backlash is on ██████████, but one thing's for sure, Twitter wants the world to #FindOur█ #WheresOur█.

Day 54: How Does a ████████████████ Retire Anyway?
Hypothetical: We have been asking ourselves this: what on █████ glorious earth could compel a ████████████ to up and ████████ without telling his country? Our best guess at the moment, if this is indeed what has occurred, it's what's done when one has no idea how to retire, and this might be how one gets oneself out of a job that, alas, one is ready to leave, theoretically.

We here at *The Exile Gazeta* are puzzling over this very █████ ███: What kind of quiet life can former authoritarians lead once they unceremoniously exit the ██████████? Do they garden and form book clubs and play cards? Or do they spend their time looking over their shoulders, and if so, then wouldn't they just stay in power since they'd have so many more ████████████████████ ████████████████████████████████? They'd have guards and blank checks and metadata and AKs and hideaways and airplanes and parades of SUVs and all that ██████.

But what if, just say, one such individual did want to retire, as a thought experiment, of course?

If they likely have all the elections cyclically rigged, it's not like they'll get voted out of power, one imagines. But say they just wanted to relax, find peace, find calm, leave the ███████, live a regular life out of the ████. Maybe it got too much. Maybe ██ ████ just wasn't really in it anymore. Maybe it got overwhelming or underwhelming. Maybe it was time to call it a day. Take up pottery. Finally write that novel. Spend more time with the grand-kids . . . .

And to that, we'd say, resign, sir, resign. No one needs the strain of ██████████ for this long. We'd say to ███████████ ████████ resign, resign, resign.

Day 50: Ghosted by Our Own ████████████ . . . Still Waiting for the Phone to Ring

We made an honest mistake, forgiving readers. In our eagerness and haste to assure you ████████████████████████ ████████████████████, we pounced too quickly to pub-lish what we genuinely believed were verified photos proving that the ████████████ was taking some kind of extended rest cure at a Norwegian spa. The evidence seemed airtight in the form of a surreptitiously captured image showing a vaporous yurt, ██ dipped into a tub (more here). There is some reliable information coming out now that these photos have been doctored, along with some damning analysis (including that it's summer in Norway, but as you see when you zoom into the image here and focus on the window, it's getting dark outside while the clock says 3:00 p.m., something our equatorially born staffers should not have missed, and we apologize).

The search, then, is on.

Day 48: EXCLUSIVE: ███ sighting confirmed!!! Scandal in Scandinavia!!!!!

Irrefutable photo evidence has been obtained by our staff of the

██ soaking in a bath of some kind. This key evidence was snapped by a concierge who knew about this lingering ████ and did us the great honor of submitting this photograph exclusively to *The Exile Gazeta*. Is there a ██████ here? And we don't mean the kind for the spa. Does this photo have plenty of evidence suggesting its ██████? The relevant details have been circled in red. Most compelling:

- A calendar showing that it is indeed ██████ of this very ███, proving this picture is current.
- The look of ███████████ in his eyes, for who would fail to recognize that?
- The flag of ██████ hanging on the wall.
- His wallet on the ledge is full of bills, as it certainly must be after all ██████████████████████████████████ ████.
- The key chain has a ███████████ charm.

Sir, if you are seeing this, first, we sincerely thank *all* of our loyal readers for their time and their flattering attention. Second, good for you for being able to digest so much ██████. We honestly didn't think you were capable. And third, we advise you to have one of your staff publish a brief official statement to end this rampant ████████, for it's very unbecoming to all involved, ourselves included, no doubt. Perhaps even something informal. If we might guide your hand, may we suggest a letter issued on your behalf along the lines of:

Dear Public,

For reasons beyond his control, the ███████████ *must cash in on his personal days. Please be assured that the country is in the adequate hands of _____ (fill in the name of preferably the deputy, if there is one now).*

At the Behest of Yours, in absentia.

Day 46: Let's Not Panic Yet (But Let's Not Not Panic, Either)

Gentle readers, the disappearance of the ███████████ is troubling news to the exile and diaspora press. Many of us write as freely as we do from around the world precisely because we know the ███████████ is over there and we are over here. We are more than a little concerned that he'll perhaps turn up in our corners of the world.

For over all these years and decades, who among us has not been tried in a court of law for simply reporting the ████, conveying ███████ as we chase down ████—no matter how hard to track, no matter how ████ or ███████? All the while offering our editorial analysis best we can? How many of us were convicted for being on Skype no matter what we said at all? Many of us have been thrown in jail for our reporting, many have been forced into ████, been ██████████, vanished along with our words? How many are too afraid to write another word? How many have ████, have ████, have been ████████ in absentia for things like ███████ ███████████████, and maybe they'll throw in disturbing ██ ██████████████████████████████████████ exposure for ███████████████ even the slightest hint of ███████ ███████ how the country is ███████. (Thank you again, loyal readers, for your letters of support through those trying trials.) We are worried—but not quite yet panicked—that our ▮▮ is on the loose and might find us in our exile, especially as our general location is publicly known. Many of the crimes we've been convicted of for our reporting are capital offenses, and so again, we are very worried, but doing our utmost not to completely lose our minds.

Please, especially for those living in the Greater Saint Paul–Minneapolis area, we at *The Exile Gazeta* would very much appreciate any news about the ▮▮▮▮▮▮▮▮'s whereabouts, especially if he is headed our way.

Day 43: Reply Requested

Dear Sir,

Your presence is requested and you are cordially invited to govern the country that has "elected" you ▮▮▮▮▮▮▮▮. Please RSVP, posthaste.

Signed,

The Editors

Day 35: On the State of the Art (and the Art of the State)

We want to explain to our readers that while other blogs have published the speculative ▮▮▮▮▮ of the disappeared ▮▮▮▮, we will refrain from doing so until we know more. So let's take a short break from this series tracing the whereabouts of the missing ▮▮▮ to issue a tangential editorial statement on the rumor that—in the long tradition of ▮▮▮▮▮▮▮▮▮—our ▮▮ has been taken to ▮▮▮▮▮▮▮▮▮ to enjoy their state-of-the-art ▮▮▮▮▮▮ and their state-of-the-art ▮▮▮▮▮▮ and their state-of-the-art ▮▮▮ ▮▮▮▮▮. If the ▮▮▮▮▮▮ of countries like ours vowed ▮▮▮▮ ▮▮▮▮▮▮▮▮▮▮▮▮▮▮▮▮ and vowed ▮▮▮▮▮▮▮ ▮▮▮▮▮▮▮▮▮▮▮▮▮▮▮▮▮▮, well then maybe we

wouldn't find ourselves in this unfortunate situation. Maybe those ██████████████████████████████, and maybe the ██████ ██████████ from those ██████████ would magically reappear.

That is all.

Day 28: Same ██, same ██

While the state media has said that the ██████████████ is fine and will be in touch with us shortly, one has to wonder, why would a ██████████go quiet for so long? Not even one public appearance, not one media roundtable or one photo-op or official statement? What's so hush-hush? Come on now. This is the same ██, same ██ . . .

And now reports are streaming in steadily from various blogs around the world. We're even seeing small notes in the global press, not front pages, mind you, but our big stories usually have to fight their way into the international "etc. summaries" as it is.

In the global blogs, though, this ordeal is getting buzz. In fact, there's a game of ping-pong going on. It started when someone in our exile blogosphere pinged some Egyptian bloggers asking if they could check if our ██ was marooned in denial/the Nile. Ha! Then two Egyptian bloggers said indeed, our ██████████ had been seen there wearing suspenders, but had departed for a language intensive at ██████████████████████ in an alpine German village. Then a German blogger rebutted that our ██████ ██████ was in Libya trying to have a séance for the ghost of ██████ ██. Some Libyan bloggers said they snooped around in ██████'s old files only to find ██████████████████████████████████ ██████████████████████████ at the Russian Space Mission just to get away from it all, but the standing space-date was canceled on account of an unexpected conflict, but perhaps another time, schedules permitting. A Russian claiming to be at the Space Center beamed down a flickering message in Morse code to a sunbather he swore was a doppelgänger relaxing on a picnic blanket on a hillside in Wales. The Welsh have yet to take the bait.

Day 26: Nothing Has ██████; Nothing Will Be ██████

Official statements are circulating informing the public that nothing has ██████; everything is ██████. As the whole spectrum of press-in-exile seems to note, this could mean anything, and therefore it ultimately has no meaning at all. Still, we are committed to sharing all we are able to gather using our modest means, and we will always tell you everything we know, no matter how incomprehensible. We are doing our best to verify everything, and we are trying to maintain some kind of journalistic standard here, even as we report on a country where the media is ██████ and official statements are ████ and simply put, the best real leads we have are rumors and gossip and speculation and, of course, ██████████. Public officials claim that nothing has ██████, but we are starting to get the feeling that nothing can ██████████.

Day 22: The Emperor Has No ██████?

Does anyone else find it more than a little odd that the ██████████ ████ has not been seen for over three weeks? Has uttered not a single ██████████? All meetings have been ██████, no sightings, no nights out on the town, no new laws or edicts. There have been no ground breakings or demolitions or speeches. Our sources even say that while the lawns of his residence are watered and the cars in his driveway still polished, the home itself looks quiet and the staff seems to be idle.

Please, thoughtful readers, write with any ████.

Day 18: EXCLUSIVE: Interview with Tailor, Barber, Cleaner of Voice for ██████!!!

As all of you must know, two and a half weeks ago at what we thought would be yet another standard state parade, the monotony was interrupted when a voice yelled out to ask our ██████████ a series of impromptu questions. Actually, these weren't questions so much as demands. Or rather, not demands, but more a mantra. Or maybe not so much a mantra as an incantation.

During this promenade, the ████████████'s same speech blared from megaphones (approx. let my great ██████ be a light guiding us into the future, blah blah blah) when this lone voice yelled out, "Give us our █████." The crowd went silent.

A real-life emperor-has-no-██████ moment, parade and all, this solitary onlooker shouted, "Our █████, our █████." And then, as if this speaker's mind wrapped around that idea, cradled it, exalted that word, the sound repeated over and over again. "Our █████, our █████, our █████." Raised arms, lifting them with each beat of "our █████, our █████, our █████." The words became a clenched fist pumping in the air, so forceful was that cry of "████████ █████ . . . ." The crowd mouthed the words, "████████████," in a silent protest.

So was born the voice for █████.

The ████████████ has not been seen since.

We were able to get a few short words with the tailor of the voice for █████, who once mended a jacket. "Bespoke, everything looks bespoke," he said. "Well spoken, bespoken."

The barber who once knew the voice for █████ ████████ issued this written statement: ████████ *impeccably groomed* ████████ *say so myself, from what I know since I offer a great service at a great rate (mention this interview and get 10% off your next service).* ████████

██

I can't really speak to that point, but they do say that ████████████
████████████████████████████████ *these things can take on the world. It's implied there in the Bible, Samson and all in a way, right, so actually, yes, I guess I can't say I'm surprised.*

The voice for ████'s cleaner said, "████████████████████ wash already smelling like roses. Like goddamn roses. Never seen anything like it, and never smelled anything like it neither. A giant, practically seven feet tall, by which I mean that's the impression ██ ███████████████████████████████ in fact. Never seen anything like it, though, that's for sure."

Clearly some part of the world is captivated, the legend is already being written for the voice who was ████████'s bell.

Day 14: Where in the World Is ████████?

As several esteemed colleagues write, our ████████████ needs three things: 1) ████, 2) ████, and 3) ████████, to be trending in the national news or the wink of a camera, the illumination of a flash, to which he appears drawn phototropically. So this much ███████████████ is not only uncharacteristic, it's literally unimaginable, unnatural, unsustainable. For whatever reason, he has gone ████, and I guarantee it is not a sudden restraint or sudden shyness or some moment of satori. Something is amiss, people.

Day 10: The Weight of Words

Everyone is talking about the voice for ████. Everyone is talking about the power of the word "████," too. The power of words. The power and physical weight of words have suddenly become an object of fascination for our community. We want to hold up words, to throw them against a wall and see if words can smash a wall, twirl those words in the air to let them take flight and maybe fly over a wall. In fact, we at *The Exile Gazeta* have been getting reports that people are chanting demands, waiting to see if they will come to life, waiting to see if their words can also work a spell on the world.

Here are a few instances that have been shared with us. We'll keep a running list going on Twitter (tweet us your observations @SaintPaulWrites4).

- Young kids waiting for snack time started chanting "recess, recess, recess," and when they were told to "please quiet down," they demanded, "peace, peace, peace" until they gently drifted off.

- A man asked a woman to marry him by getting down on one knee and chanting, "say yes, say yes, say yes." The woman felt the words travel from him to her shoulders, then flutter against her neck, up her cheek, to her lips, that parted to say "kiss, kiss, kiss."

- A lonely taxi driver was lost and had no bars on his cell phone, so he chanted, "reception, reception, reception," and he came across a small motel where the receptionist gave him a map and her number.

- A former vocalist waiting for the bus sang the word "brava, brava, brava" in such a high pitch she broke the glasses of a passerby who turned out to be her first singing coach. Impressed, the coach invited her to star in his next production.

- A migrant laborer separated from his family for fifteen years by several countries and not the right papers began chanting the word "please, please, please," and when he got to his apartment that night, a letter was waiting approving his application, finally allowing him to visit his wife and children.

Day 7: Where Has Our Media ▉▉▉▉▉ Gone?

Have we ever had a full week without hearing from our outspoken ▉? He's not been making appearances or enjoying banquets with the many ▉▉▉▉▉ always at his doorstep. He's not met with any ▉▉▉▉▉▉▉, not headed up any ▉▉▉▉▉▉. In fact, he bailed on the big ▉▉▉▉▉▉▉ just this past week, which has got to be a first for ▉▉ who's been called such an "articulate articulator of ▉▉▉▉▉▉▉" by some (we at *The Exile Gazeta* reiterate that we see him as a symbol of ▉▉▉▉, but that's another matter that you can find plenty written about by our staffers <u>here</u> and <u>here</u> and <u>here</u> and also <u>here</u> and of course <u>here</u> and <u>here</u> and <u>here</u> as well, and not to mention <u>here</u> and <u>here</u>).

The buzz is that his disappearance is all due to the events that transpired at the monumental parade when the voice for ▉▉▉ called him out (more <u>here</u>). True, while that event must have filled the ▉▉ with ▉▉▉ and ▉▉▉▉▉▉, can that alone explain why ▉▉▉▉▉▉ would go off the grid like this?

That would seem far-fetched, except . . .

. . . except that this might have been the first time the ▉▉▉ ▉▉▉▉ has had to face public protest head on. He's ▉▉▉▉▉ opposition in the country for so long that the sound of dissent must be new to him. It perhaps was so unfamiliar and so jarring, it was an assault to what must be such delicate eardrums.

What must it feel like to hear criticism for the first time, and in front of the whole world? Let this be a lesson to all that it is better to thicken the skin by letting critiques trickle in as they arise rather than to thin the skin so that one small ██████████ cuts to the bone.

The Voice for ████

For those lucky enough to be in the crowd at this year's parade, all we can say is that we were stunned watching online, and we were thrilled to hear this singular voice pose such bold questions directly to the ██████████. Perhaps the boldest and most critical questions ever posed directly to the ██████████.

Everyone is talking about "the voice for ████." Surely you have heard of this voice? Surely you know about this voice, whose echo can still be felt circling the world. It was as if, until ████ was returned, there was nothing to do but to call out for it. Language started and stopped there, and nothing more and nothing less and nothing else could be said except "████."

So heavy was that word that the ██████████ seemed to retreat into the folds of history, almost disappearing before everyone's very eyes. Some were saying the voice for ████ would take down all of authoritarianism, too. Imagine that, if one voice calling out a simple ideal could be a revolution in itself.

Is autocracy that fragile that a word said just so could challenge its power, make it vanish on site? Only time will tell.

The Life and Times of the
Little Manuscript & Anonymous

1. The Little Manuscript

I am somehow reminded of a rumor about an ill-fated manuscript I read about in the diaspora blogs. I heard more of the story from Ephraim, who got the scoop from Henoch, but we all suspect Aster and Benyam were the primary sources.

By publishing standards, this was a lucky manuscript at first glance. The manuscript sat on the desk of the Ministry of Culture for less than a day before it was read, embraced, fawned over. "It will be called 'the little manuscript' to show it is humble," said one bureaucrat, and no one in the room objected. The little manuscript found itself petted, held up to the light, instantly lauded by lowly operatives and their bosses and bosses' bosses alike. As it was passed along, the little manuscript inspired handshakes, made a slew of alliances—all accidental—and became pleased but confused.

It turned out, to the surprise of the little manuscript, a hard to fathom sleight of hand would occur among the higher-ups. First keep in mind that the little manuscript told about the horrors of the country's history, the old Soviet-backed regime that reigned terror during the Cold War right up until communism fell, and the unhealed scar it left in the people and, it seemed, in the land itself. The little manuscript was therefore very good for the higher-ups. How helpful to have all of this remembering of the awful past going on because it had been a long time since any of the rulers had come to power, a long time since they'd been welcomed as agents of change, and they were afraid people would forget! They feared that people would ask, "What are you still doing there in power? What about the rest of us who wouldn't mind some power, too, huh?" How nice to have something to point to in order to say without saying, "But look what we did, what freedoms we bestowed, what we saved our beloved country from—surely we deserve this power still!"

And there was an election going on (and that's a whole other story). And then there's the simple fact that governments are made up of regular humans, and humans are inclined to make themselves look good. Certainly nothing could make them look quite so good as a manuscript that described the country in the grips of hell, and then painted them as saviors, even if by chains of deduction and transitive logic.

The little manuscript was made to look good, too. The little manuscript was personally brought to the printer by the PM's top aide. It was copied on beautiful paper and artfully bound. It was tickled to win every prestigious award and even a few brand new ones from various national agencies before the press had a chance to cool, was adapted for film and television by the National Broadcasting Channel starring popular actors and with top-notch publicity.

The shy author, who was a woman of simple living, and who had an almost painful aversion to crowds, was bewildered to find that she had become a star. More alarming to her was that without any process, greasing, pleading, or mischief, her tiny one-room live/work studio had been upgraded and she was moved to the top floor of one of the luxurious new government developments popping up across town. Considering the years she'd waited to finally get on the housing list to begin with, it was doubly unbelievable. On top of this, she'd been given a staff and a stipend by an anonymous benefactor, though all her checks were return-addressed to the Ministry of Information. She was a guest of honor at award ceremonies throughout the country and ushered around from place to place as a VVIP. She found herself wearing a ball gown once or twice, which she'd never done before in her fifty-five years. She was troubled by these unforeseen turns, but how could she say no to any of this? She couldn't possibly offend all these powerful people, could she? Oh, how she was trapped, and all this newfound power had made her more powerless than ever. What a strange path my life has taken, she marveled. I've literally written myself into a corner!

Things quickly got stranger for the shy author and her little manuscript. Beloved by the powerful, they quickly became hated by the opposition to the powerful. Some members of the opposition started mumbling then grumbling then whispering then chanting then shouting then bellowing that the author had it all wrong, and that this little manuscript was overblown. They said the past had not been all that bad, and that the rulers now therefore were not so great, by inference. This was right before the polls would open and all kinds of lines were being read between, all kinds of stories were being rewritten or reclaimed in various acts of larceny. It was a free-for-all as narratives were fought over, stolen, retold for political gain. In the midst of all the looting, this little manuscript had become so much more than a little manuscript, much more than a historical account, a record of those hard times. The little manuscript found itself in the middle of a tug-of-war as political interests tried to take control of the story, tried to interpret history to their own benefit. Holding one end of the rope were those who doted over the little manuscript's literary contributions of the very highest merit, and holding the other end of the rope were those who could only see a reviled scrap of propaganda. The little manuscript was pulled apart, pieced together, and ended up as fodder in many fires (real and ideological), and it grew quite exhausted. I'm not cut out for this, thought the little manuscript.

Worse off was the little manuscript's author, who was overwhelmed with disbelief, and was becoming nervous—a nervous wreck. Not a politician but an artist, not ideologue but an aesthete, she had been simply unprepared. She sat in her glamorous office with its beautiful view, her overeducated, too good-looking staff, and hid.

But during all this time, something else was happening to the little manuscript, something unseen by the author. The little manuscript was on its way to becoming something different altogether as soon as it had been purchased by someone who came to be known as Reader X. Reader X was so surprised to find such an intimate story about the anguish of a history he'd endured but repressed—the pain of torture, the terrors of executions, the fear of hunger, the heartbreak of disappearances, the sadness that siphoned off part of the lifeblood of that time in his youth, forming a new artery that seeped into the darkness and caused his heart to skip a beat at regular intervals. Upon finishing the little manuscript, Reader X felt his heartbeat flutter as a tear welled up in his eye, then another, then another, and he cried for quite a while. This story reminds me of what I went through, Reader X thought. After the tears, Reader X felt a knot in his back burst like a bubble, then another, then another, like he was floating on little glorious explosions that rid him of a layer of past. He told his friends and neighbors, passed the book along to his brothers and sisters, and they also had similar experiences of tears and bubbles. He told his colleagues about the little manuscript, and those readers told other readers about the little manuscript, whose reach propelled this tide of renewing and releasing.

Then there was another twist, but this wouldn't take place until, oh, late the next year. Someone known as Reader Zero encountered the little manuscript, and felt so connected to it that she wrote her own manuscript about her own experience of this history, memories, family stories, accounts gathered from libraries, dinner tables, dreams. Then Reader Zero's friend, Reader One, wrote his own account. Then a family wrote their own, and then another and another. Each new manuscript inspired more and more, and more and more burdensome memories and hidden-away pasts popped like soapsuds across the city. Readers 10, 12, 14 all wrote their own manuscripts, and a cluster of their readers did the same. And these were also passed around, and also made the neighborhood lighter. As for the powerful, they thought things were working quite well, that they really lucked out with the way that this story was being so beautifully and organically perpetuated. They basked in the reflected shine.

But the powerful didn't see what was coming next. The little manuscript had, beneath their very eyes, eventually grown so big that no one could own this story, claim this history. The past was a story about the people in their own voice. Operatives wondered if they'd ever again be able to use this history for votes, legitimacy, legacy, ideology. They wondered if the story of the little manuscript had gotten out of hand; belonged to too many. It seemed to not only have taken on a life of its own but had given a new life to so many.

It took about another eighteen months before the shy author heard about this effect, and became happy. Then, inspired, she decided to write a second manuscript about the multitude of manuscripts and their triumph over political interests, how politicians couldn't control the country's story, but that the real history of the country belonged to them all. The shy author finished this second manuscript, and there was another election then (but that's a whole other story), and the second manuscript sat on the desk of the Minister of Culture for less than an hour before it was circulated within the whole bureau. This time, though, the party grew very angry with the shy author. This second manuscript did not make any one of them look good. In fact, it made them look downright dirty.

The shy author's neighbors and friends were astonished. They couldn't believe she'd written such a story! Didn't she know to keep quiet? It was dangerous to be so bold in this country! But the shy author whispered, what can I do? I'm a writer. Stories come to mind, and I express them as best I can. I'm not even always sure I'm the one in charge at all, the pen conspiring with the page sometimes guides the way. I only have so much control.

Some friends understood; some thought she was mad. All thought she was impractical. Stop being a writer, they begged. What will I do? she asked them. There's always business school, they responded. In any case, the shy author's awards were confiscated, her staff fired. She lost her office/apartment, fled the city, ducked away to a remote village in the south, and stayed there until the end of that month. I lost track of her after that.

2. Anonymous

On election day, like any day, the morning fog disappears into the mountaintops that seem to inhale it like cigarette smoke, taking in the damp night air just before the dawn. The muezzin switches on his microphone with an easy flick and summons a cry that has lodged in his larynx like a sob-choked protest. He bellows and the sound echoes through the air, born with cries as well as wings, like any birth. The wealthy merchants live far from the pungent city center, but their employees lift themselves out of bed and walk into the side streets that branch from the market. They line up outside a one-stall bathroom, remove their slippers, roll up their sleeves, lift their hems or cuff their pants. One by one they enter the wet room and fill their water bottles, wash, spread mats on the street, face Mecca in the darkness, and bow deep, sometimes bruising their foreheads against the rhythm of prayer.

Down the road, the cathedral doors are unlocked and men and women stop in on the way to work. They kneel, give alms, ask their sins to be lifted. They sit and listen to the mezmur music, the steady church chanting lulling them to sleep again for a minute or two. They pause at the altars set beneath the windows. The sky is blue now, and the votives' modest light gently brightens the cavernous alcoves. Tin-backed candelabras enhance this diminutive light, as if to say, after all, this is why light exists, not to stand opposite the dark, but to engage it, to confront the fuzzy border that we call dawn on the one hand and dusk on the other. Parishioners light candles, mumble quick prayers, step onto streets whose cobblestones are covered with mucky water that reflects the rising sun, transmitting and expanding the soft early rays of day, reflecting and refracting the meager glint of dawn.

Ephraim moves quickly through this sleepy scene, passes the market stalls that are just starting to open, and hurries back to his motel, where he'll have to wait for his bed to empty. He accepts that he gets what he pays for in this tucked-away four-room space where beds go for the cost of a top-shelf drink, mostly to one-night wards. There are several longer-term renters, including Ephraim, who has been here for three days straight and sleeps in his bed during the day, earning back the expense by renting it again for the evenings. Because of this habit, the manager, Zena, immediately regarded Ephraim as being a bit of an oddball, albeit one with a strong constitution. How else could he never request fresh linens, never ask that his mattress be turned, or the pillows switched out after God knew what was done on the bed, on the mattress, between those sheets the night before? The other tenants, thinking of what they themselves did, or saw done, or planned or wished to do, regard him with even greater wonder.

That morning, a young man of maybe eighteen is sleeping on Ephraim's bed, so peacefully in fact that Ephraim doesn't disturb him, but just sits on the floor leaning against the wall. There's an empty bed on the other side of the room, but it's not his to claim. The other two tenants who share the room don't stir, having stumbled in only hours before. Ephraim hears the crackle of coffee roasting next door, and the swish of morning chores, and he begins to think about his estranged wife whom he desperately wishes would do him the small favor of acknowledging all the charming reasons she fell in love with him in the first place. That is to say, he is daydreaming of his past and all he's given up.

Beyond the window where Zena is washing dishes, a modest line is about to form. Lucas has taken the early bus from the central depot, disembarking when he feels the more expensive part of the city receding into something along the lines of what he can afford. At the same time, Yacob also makes his way to this spot, also seeking an escape for similar reasons as Ephraim: a moment of respite, a minute of anonymity, to just be left alone, out of sight, and as of late, away from fear. Yacob reaches the gate just before

Lucas, though Lucas was seated slightly in front of Yacob on the bus. Zena opens the front gate tossing the bucket of soapy water onto the sidewalk and the two men approach, loudly and urgently competing for her attention. Zena retains her composure, and though she stands still, she gives the impression of shaking her pointed finger at the men as she informs them there is one—and only one—bed for the night. They'll have to fight it out, she says, and leaves them to their battle.

Zena checks in on the one and only empty bed in the motel. She says a quiet hello to Ephraim, and shimmies past him on tiptoe so as not to awake the other guests. Ephraim calls out to her, softly, "When it's available, please could you bring me a copy of the evening *Gazette*?" She nods. "And coffee along with dinner tonight," he adds, as he takes out a pen.

Nothing ever changes, nothing is the same, Ephraim writes in his journal. He places it in his bag with such satisfaction, as if he's captured the zeitgeist of the day in that one line. Without waking his subletter, Ephraim straightens out the items on his nightstand, his rosary, a worn copy of the orthodox Bible, a large wooden cross that he has placed next to his bed because he knows that an ostentatious show of faith will effectively preempt any unwanted questions from his roommates. Certainly, they would look at this iconography and become instantly comforted that they'd seen the likes of him before.

The rest of his luggage remains in stow. In the deepest recess of his bag, his treasures lay buried. Beneath a false bottom, he has hidden a folder in which he recorded notes for articles that he always wished he could publish but never has. There is a small satchel of food that his now-estranged wife, Helen, prepared for him before he left home earlier in the week: dried meat, fruit, bread, "things that keep," she said between bitter tirades that made him realize his marriage was finally truly and irredeemably at risk.

She'd take a breath after berating him and then interject a little wisdom. "Always take something with you to eat, and always eat before you leave the house," Helen had said the last time he saw her, as she had been saying for ages. "Once you walk out the door, you never know when you'll be able to eat again." Words he had taken lightly in his younger days, and had smiled at dismissively for so many years now, bore the weight of his precarious reality.

His reality being that he'd ruined his easy life just four days ago, but he was practically forced to do it, like someone had held a gun to his head and made him pull the trigger, is what he told Helen. She said, "No one made you do this thing you did to yourself and to us," even though that's not how it felt to him. Four days ago, Ephraim went to his usual bar to finish writing a story about the election. Sure, the election hadn't happened yet, but he could still get in his assignment early. He knew what to say. He knew to write that the vote was won in a landslide by the incumbent party. He knew to write that the whole country was overjoyed by the win, that massive crowds took to the streets to cheer the victory, that the people had spoken and their voice had been heard. He'd write that on account of this affirmation of democracy, the market would skyrocket, criminals would cower, and though it couldn't be proved, it seemed that even the water was a little crisper and the honey a little sweeter on a day like this. Everything, which was already great, would somehow be greater, was what Ephraim knew he was supposed to say.

It wasn't the first time he'd dialed one in early, nor was it even the second time he wrote a story before it happened. He'd learned he could file articles hours, days, sometimes weeks ahead of an event. He wrote about the last election a month before it happened, an embellished story about how peaceful the vote had been, how bright the leaders shone, how enlightened the result was, how wonderful for everyone that the powers that be would serve another five years. Best of all, Ephraim got paid early, cashed in his checks, and took a month-long vacation to Zanzibar.

He'd hit upon a winning formula, but when Ephraim sat down with his pen and paper at the bar several days ago, he felt a weariness settle in as he wrote the words he knew were expected of him. He recalled the little manuscript he'd just finished reading, and wished he could write something authentic, too. Maybe he could write it and just not turn it in? He wondered, would that make a difference to anyone in the world? If a tree falls in the forest and no one is there to hear it, does it make a sound? He could turn it in to his editor, who would see it along with the censors and whomever else in the government would track him down and arrest him. If a tree falls in the forest and a handful of corrupt bureaucrats hear it, does it make a sound?

As Ephraim tried to put down on paper what he knew he was supposed to write, his pen resisted his hand. Then, as if possessed by the pen itself, Ephraim found himself crossing out the predictable version of his article and starting over to write the truth as he saw it. He could barely keep up as the pen raced along; he wrote that the people were afraid to speak their minds amid all the meaningless arrests and disappearances that happened over the course of months, years, maybe even decades, centuries, who can say? Then there were the newspaper closures, the forced internet outages, the censorship laws, the policies that made people speak under their breath when they expressed hardly anything at all, threatening to turn the citizenry into a country of whisperers. He wrote, *We may never know the true vote count, or if the vote was ever even counted. One thing is clear, there were no winners today, for unless something changes, we will all be doomed to repeat this day over and over every five years, and that's a loss for each of us.* He did what he felt had to be done, said what he felt had to be said, maybe just to show he was an independent human being who could chew his own food, and brush his own teeth, and tie his own shoes, and think his own thoughts. Then he decided not to tuck the story into obscurity, but to submit it to his editor, for no matter the sound, who's to say what can't be toppled by a falling tree? When it came time to enter the byline, he signed it "Anonymous," paused, exed that out—his pen conspiring with him, pressing his bravest words into the paper: his own name.

He proceeded to get rather drunk and stumbled out of the bar, stumbled out of a taxi and stumbled into the empty press room, dropped off the article and his office keys, and stumbled home dumbfounded and at a loss, like he was walking out a dark room and into a bright harsh oblivion, white like a blank page. He'd blame it on the beer when Helen asked him what he was thinking writing what he did. I wasn't thinking, he'd say, and only he and his pen would know different.

The morning after, in the unforgiving equatorial light, he came to terms with what he'd done and told Helen he'd be going away. Ephraim's name would have been turned in to authorities by now, and so he ate a big breakfast cooked by his angry and fearful and screaming and soon-to-be-estranged wife before he took off for this unremarkable motel where he tucked himself away, sneaking off during nights to plan an escape, coming back to sleep off his exhaustion at dawn. Maybe Ephraim would find a way to go to Europe or America. Jail was a possibility; he could see himself ending up in prison or even worse if he was unlucky. He'd escape if he was saved, silenced either way, silenced for now, anyway.

* * *

As he contemplates how finding his voice has led him to lose it completely, Ephraim hears a squabble outside escalating, and can just make out the words.

"Yes, today is technically election day," Yacob concedes as he leans against the bus stop sign, "but what does that have anything to do with why the last bed should go to you?"

Lucas rubs the arc of his nose, theatrically. "I'm an election monitor here for the vote. I need someplace to stay, to put my things down before I go do my job."

Yacob shakes his head and says, "First of all, why don't you grasp what this is for you? Why don't you understand this is your day off? Go on, you've earned it! Or maybe you haven't earned it, but you should take it. You should be at the movies or the beach— go spend a few days in Mombasa. I mean, you'll say the election was 'free and fair' so your job is already done. What are you even doing here? Why not go treat yourself?" Yacob doesn't let the question land. "Second, you're an election monitor just temporarily, yes? Well, I am who I am for good. I mean, do you know who I am?"

Lucas squints and inches toward Yacob, who wears sunglasses and a big hat. "I couldn't say you look familiar," Lucas responds earnestly.

"What an absurd, absurd position for a man of my standing," Yacob says to Lucas. "Although of course being able to go incognito is a luxury to a man like me," he adds. Yacob opts for another language, takes out his wallet and peels off a few bills to bribe Lucas to let him take the bed. Lucas is suspicious. "If you have this kind of money, what are you doing here?" Lucas asks, pocketing the cash. Yacob, thinking his payoff has bought some peace and silence, turns his back on Lucas, calling for Zena.

When Zena opens the gate for Yacob, she offers coffee or tea. "No," he grumbles, hoping that she recognizes him and simultaneously also that he would remain unknown. Zena shows him the empty bed without fanfare, and he is self-conscious. This sudden anonymity is, he knows, an inevitability he himself invited, like enduring the fallout of an obviously doomed relationship. It didn't have to end this way, and yet, it was bound to end badly. He should have known better, he thinks to himself.

Before he had published his last novel, Yacob was not only the latest darling of the country's literary world, but one of its few remaining public figures. He had gained instant fame upon writing a book that, on second thought, seemed "remarkably familiar," said the censors. Still, the national reviews were good, his confidence inflated, Yacob embarked on a ten-city book tour to promote *The Merchant of Menace*. The tour was a mild success, though a few attendees would casually ask, usually within the first ten minutes of Q&A, didn't it seem like this had all been done before? With the earnings from his debut, Yacob invested in a new press, mostly to publish his own books, and from there, the sky was the limit. His second work, *A Tale of Three Cities*, was also met with cautious approval by the censors, who couldn't quite put their fingers on their sense of déjà vu, but still, it passed their requirements, a square peg in a square hole. It was widely read, and well liked. Several other moderate successes quickly followed: *Love in a Time of Famine, Notes from the Basement*. He began to get his friends to write good reviews, and so his ego never took a hit, nor did his bank account. By the time this prolific streak ground to a halt, Yacob had written no less than fifteen books and had become a millionaire, a rare local accomplishment in general, unheard of for a writer.

It wasn't until Yacob took three years to write an original work that his career as a writer—and as a public citizen—became seriously threatened before it was completely shattered. He had read an inspiring little manuscript that moved him to try to write the truth, the whole truth, and only the truth. This little manuscript compelled him to compose what he hoped would be a great contemporary novel about the plight of his people, their hardships as farmers and as urban toilers, the toll these precarious livelihoods took on their bodies and souls, what it meant to be alive in this time and this place. His mother, his wife, his wife's mother, his manager, agent, brothers, cousins, all told him there are things that are not talked about in the nation these days. Like the whole truth, that was one of the things, they told him, as if he didn't already know. Just keep on doing what he'd been doing, they begged, the tried and tested and pre-approved. Swelled by his previous successes and inspired for once in his life, Yacob felt entitled to his freedom. Yacob listened to these advisors but paid no real attention and published *Anonymous*, about the plight of the everyman, a book no one read except for a few censors who confiscated every last copy and locked them up somewhere within the Ministry of Information.

Yacob was working on a new book now, *Chronicle of an Exile Foretold*, hoping that the path that took him from the most expensive, most heavily gated community in the capital to the courtyard of this dingy little motel where he had to fight to rent a bed for the cost of a cheap beer was not a one-way road.

The day comes and goes. Yacob revises *Chronicle of an Exile Foretold*, and Ephraim is about to forfeit his bed to another subletter while the evening tapers off, no real disruptions to speak of. As the sun traces its parabolic climb, the news of the vote seems to fade away unseen, finished almost before it begins. Dusk seems to sneak up on them all as Zena comes around with coffee and the evening *Gazette* for Ephraim, who takes the paper and laughs at the front page. The banner headline reads, "Today's Election a Resounding Success." He recognizes the story immediately, the very one he'd printed five years ago, with a few tweaks here and there, like the date, some names, and the weather and the roster of A-listers who called to congratulate the winning party members on their reelection. The paper ran the same old quotes from the anonymous independent monitors who praised the result, and the story had the same old quotes from the anonymous ministers who said democracy had come to stay in their fair country, the same old quotes from anonymous professors and from anonymous grateful mothers and anonymous ecstatic businessmen and anonymous schoolchildren. One of the only changes to the piece was that Ephraim hasn't been credited. The byline reads "Anonymous," and Ephraim wonders what that means for him. He also wonders if maybe one day, maybe his shelved story would appear in the histories if not in the news. But that day is not today, which is already slipping away.

Faint echoes of the last calls to prayer die out, the priest and muezzin flick off their microphones amid the fading echo of their proclamations, and the city, glowing yellow, quiets to dusty blue before the final glint of sun creeps behind the landscape, and the fog falls down the hills once more.

The Elders

Where and into what circumstances a person is born is an act of fate, but where they're laid to rest is meant to tell the story of a life, what it has all led to. And after the tragic end that took Engineer Paulos from this world, he deserved to be buried with great thought and care. But even with weeks of thoughtful, careful deliberation, his community still couldn't decide where that should be—Texas, where he'd lived twenty years, or his birthplace of Ethiopia? With no next of kin, his anxious neighbors were left to decide. So passionately did the community want to do right by Engineer Paulos that they fought over his remains in a tug of war that had him languishing in the purgatory of the morgue for nearly a month now. It would soon be time to come together again to mourn forty days of his passing without him being laid to rest. That just wouldn't do. He couldn't idle there any longer, what with his soul to tend to, not to mention his earthly being. The only option left was to convene a revered council of elders to settle the question, and thus interpret

Engineer Paulos' life, frame it with meaning, and immortalize its closing lines.

The first person who'd be tapped for this daunting challenge was Mrs. Sarah, who was invited to take part not for her good judgment, but to avoid, preemptively, the firestorm she'd set loose if she were left out of such an important decision. Better that the community go to her with heads bowed, pleading that she lend her wisdom to the occasion. She'd tell them she'd consider it, she'd promise to consult her schedule, ask for more time as she hemmed and hawed, all the while boasting about the invitation, wondering aloud whether she should accept, which she'd do of course, eventually. "If I can be of any small service" would be how she'd put it.

Liya and her brother Aaron would be asked, too. They were key to solving the most difficult disputes the community had faced, ones that the other elders didn't want to tackle: the marriage of Kia and Negash and the crisis of the church organ. Kia and Negash's romance in itself was harmless, though Kia's father, Stephanos, thought Negash wasn't good enough for Kia, who was beautiful, shrewd, and a remarkable cook, the ultimate triple threat in her father's eyes. But beyond this, Stephanos and Negash's mother, Ife, had fought over who controlled the water well that straddled their yards back in Ethiopia, though everyone knew (though it couldn't be said) that the fight was really about how Ife had agreed to date Stephanos before she had a shotgun wedding to a traveling salesman. This left Stephanos so heartbroken and bitter that he married the next girl who came along, divorced her just as fast, and ended up bouncing around the country, sending postcards to Ife to get a rise out of her, though she was busy tending to her newborn son. And still for decades, even when he lived hundreds of miles away, Stephanos fought with Ife over the water well whose diameter was traced exactly by their property line. At first, Ife's husband conceded to Stephanos's demands—buying new masonry, checking the sulfur levels in the water—but when Ife's husband passed away, Ife decided to fight back. Stephanos issued more challenges, and Ife loudly protested them one by one. They just wouldn't let the fight subside, even when the well had run out of water, even when it was cemented over so no one would accidentally fall into the defunct structure. The well was dry, but Stephanos spouted one complaint after another, and Ife did the same. After they left Ethiopia and coincidentally moved to the same community in Texas, they still spat under their breaths about that well every time they passed each other. And now Stephanos's daughter wanted to marry Ife's son. Well, it wouldn't do.

Kia and her father and Negash and his mother were rounded up and visited by Liya and Aaron, the revered elders who would settle the argument. They listened carefully, and like everyone, the elders could see that with this dispute, the destination was clear, but the road to get there was not. The elders devised a plan: They insisted that before the children could be married, Stephanos should ask Ife to dinner, for the sake of the children, for the sake of bringing stability and harmony to the families, if not in this generation, then in the next. Let the two warring parents sit down, for their progeny, and break some bread and have some wine and forge a kind of conclusion. Ife and Stephanos had that dinner and were married along with Negash and Kia in a double ceremony where Liya and Aaron sat in the front row, the matter of the water well evaporating quite swiftly after some thirty-two years.

The question of the church organ was even more difficult to solve because it divided the whole community. Not that there was a church, only a desire for a church and a ten-year vision in the works, still everyone took a side on the question of whether it should be designed to hold an organ. One camp argued that there was no mention of an organ in the Bible, so it couldn't have a place in this house of God. But there was no mention of electricity or indoor plumbing in the Bible either, said the other camp. What would you have people do, pray in the dark and piss in the rose-bushes? Anyway, wouldn't it draw in a younger, more assimilated crowd who were surely being tempted to other churches because of their organs? The younger, assimilated crowd must learn the old traditions, rebutted the first camp. And on and on it went. Liya and Aaron were consulted, and they proposed that the instrument not be played until *after* the service was complete, and then, when the congregation was eating and catching up, it would be nice to have a little organ music to enjoy over lunch since a stereo was clearly out of the question—a point on which everyone agreed.

Liya, Aaron, and Mrs. Sarah were at the core of the group of elders most often called for the impossible challenges, with variations due to availability, conflicts of interest, and so on. Two more were added because of the seriousness of the task regarding Engineer Paulos. The community chose Sesi, who was restless and would move things along. Unchecked, a dilemma like this might lead to endless stalemate, and the community couldn't allow that. Sesi was hardly able to sit still for more than a couple hours, so he was just what they needed in the form of a walking, talking timer. They passed over Solomon, who was brilliant but people sensed deep down that he made calculated decisions to protect his status in the community and couldn't be trusted to prioritize even Engineer Paulos over his many other personal interests. Instead, they chose the mediator, Adam, because he could see every side to a situation: the good, the bad, the this and the that, and find a way forward, no matter how narrow the path. He was the one who got everyone to come together after their small garage turned community center burned to the ground. Some speculated the fire was set out of hate, some speculated it was random chance, though everyone felt uneasy. Adam worried over where his community would meet on Sundays to pray and to bond now that their center was ashes, but his friend Joshua the rabbi mentioned the synagogue was empty on Sundays. Joshua opened the synagogue doors to the Ethiopian community every week asking nothing in return, and Adam's prominence grew for helping secure a solution in a trying situation.

Adam became the de facto leader of the community, and so he was the one to give the announcements at the weekly convening that Sunday when Engineer Paulos's case would be brought. Adam mentioned that the health fair would be next week, offering cholesterol and blood pressure screenings, that the contribution of community dues was up by 10 percent, and also congratulations to this year's graduates, who were called to stand beside him and take in the riotous applause. Then, after he read through the town's weekly events list—a concert at the local café featuring a free tortilla-making class, the town's 5k fun run benefiting the library, and an outdoor screening of *Urban Cowboy*, Adam summoned the other elders to join him as they deliberated the lasting fate of Engineer Paulos.

It was a formidable council of elders, who together had lived 510 years, seen thirty-five droughts, fifty-two floods, fifteen famines, and most important for these purposes, countless births and deaths. As they all stood together by the podium, they heard the whispers from those around them about the questions they were being asked to weigh, about belonging, about country, about acceptance, about inclusion and exclusion, tolerance and intolerance—that is, about love and hate.

Adam began, "And so we are here to decide the most serious question of where a man—Engineer Paulos—should be laid to rest.

And in so doing, we must consider the even more serious question of where he was embraced, where he belonged? For we are born into a family, a nation, a station in life, and all of that is decided by powers beyond us. But we settle back into the earth on ground of our own choosing, within constraints. If the circumstances of Engineer Paulos's passing had been different, something natural, say, then there would be no question to deliberate—his final resting place would be just down the road in the local cemetery. But the facts being what they are, we have to consider whether he'd want to spend eternity tied to this land rather than the cradle of his first home. Let me hand the question over to the Sesi first," Adam said as Sesi was impatiently inching closer to Adam, waiting for him to wrap up.

"They called us defectors back then," bellowed Sesi, who'd come to the US as a refugee during the early Derg era. Those in Sesi's cohort were revered by the community, the early arrivals, the pioneers who paved the way. So when Sesi spoke, the crowd listened, as they'd been listening to Sesi all along. "We were held up as champions back then for our daring escapes, we defectors. We the idealists, brave believers in freedom, apostates who managed to evade the Iron Curtain, physically, ideologically. Back when I arrived, they'd set aside space here specifically for those fleeing the Communist Bloc. Back then, they held open the door for us, the defectors. Sheltered us, protected us, the defectors, back then. Back then, we the defectors were accepted, were we not? We were defectors then. And now? Does anyone else feel betrayed?"

The crowd gasped when Sesi threw up his hands and pounded them down on the lectern.

"Does anyone else feel lied to? Suddenly, we're objects of fear and hate and paranoia now? We have been deceived. And Engineer Paulos has been deceived by a different lie. His lie was the one about bringing your hardworking, capable people and they will thrive. That was the lie they fed him. He didn't give up on it either, even when things were hard. Like when the oil company laid him off during the recession, what did he do? He found a job as a janitor during the days, tutored kids in math after school for free, and then worked on his own projects at night, keeping hope that one day he'd find work he loved again. Yet it's all cut short because those men aimed their frustration at our dear Engineer Paulos. Their intolerance, racism, and betrayal is unspeakable. I have been lied to and Engineer Paulos has been lied to, and I have no patience for that. I say he should be sent back to Ethiopia to be buried there where he at least was never betrayed by the kind of falsehoods on which a man builds his whole life and loses it, too."

There was a murmur in the audience as an angry Sesi walked to a chair, nodding his head at the words he'd just spoken, looking up so the chill of the chamber could dry the tears that he was surprised were welling now—he thought he'd shed them all already over the fate of Engineer Paulos. Sesi heard snippets from those before him, whispering to their neighbors.

"I feel a little betrayed, too, in a way."

"Most people in the US are not like the thugs who attacked Engineer Paulos."

"Everyone lies."

"The story I was told about this country was about bringing huddled masses."

"We can't let the people who harmed Engineer Paulos define this whole country."

Liya had arrived at the podium by now, and she cut short the talk with a loud chant of "No, no, no, no, no!" Followed by, "No!"

She turned to Sesi and stomped her foot and hollered, "No, no, no, no, no!"

She turned to the gathered and cried out, "No!"

She stepped back, and she combed her bright white hair back out of her eyes with both hands. She rubbed her hands together and leaned them on the podium, shifting her weight forward, closing her eyes. She whispered, "No." Then began, "No, he is not going anywhere. No, no, no! Engineer Paulos was an American. A Texan. He moved here twenty years ago to work in the local branch of a global oil company by his own free will. He'd been an employee in their Nigerian office, and then in their Alaskan one before finding himself in this border town near the Gulf of Mexico that he'd never heard of until he got his transfer, which he chose to accept. As luck would have it, he came to us. I think it was Mrs. Sarah who heard about his arrival through the grapevine," Liya said, looking at Mrs. Sarah, who nodded matter-of-factly, and everyone knew she'd be willing to take the credit whether it was hers to claim or not. "Because of Mrs. Sarah, we knew to be ready for his arrival, waiting with advice, with food, with lots of questions. He struck me as so polite and accommodating.

"And as Sesi said, we all remember when he lost his job during the Great Recession and started volunteering long hours around town wondering what he would do next. The thing is, he was American now, his center had shifted after all this time. He did not go anywhere, but kept on right here. As most of us know, it was through his volunteering that he started to see a need and realized he could open his own consultancy to help businesses in the area. And so Sesi, you forgot to mention that before he became a janitor, he opened up his shop, he hired and trained a team, and was loved by his employees and our small immigrant community, and resented by many others, we now know. And some people just wouldn't—just couldn't—let him succeed, not without a fight. And even when he was driven out of business by their slander about his untrustworthiness as an outsider, he closed his shop and Engineer Paulos became the school janitor. Where? Right here in this country—he did not go anywhere. And I heard it said that when Engineer Paulos got home after his shift as a janitor and after tutoring the kids, he'd worked hard on his inventions and hoped one of them would lead to something. And whether or not that was true, he never stopped trying to find a place where he fit here, and he never stopped believing in the promise that brought him here. He did not run away on account of the actions of some bad people. In the end, what those who resented him did to him is unthinkable, unutterable. The vile words they defaced his body with using, what is that called, spray paint? Spray paint that we all tried to wash off his skin, but could not? Those hateful, unrepeatable words might follow him to his grave, but his commitment to this country should be with him always, too.

"We would send the wrong message if we laid our friend to rest anywhere other than here. We would be saying that they won. We would concede defeat. On the other hand, we would send the right message to keep him right here. We would be telling the world that he held his ground. That we all are standing our ground. And if it means we have to keep vigil over his tombstone to make sure the perpetrators—and let's hope they are caught one day—don't continue to defile the body and memory of Engineer Paulos, then that's what we'll do. We'll watch over his grave and care for him in the afterlife just as we tried to do in the here and now."

Liya's pronouncement got a light applause, a flicker of fingertips on palms as people were fired up but also solemn. Her brother

Aaron took over next and waited for the clapping to subside. He leaned his aching hands on the lectern to relieve the pressure on his aching back and wrapped his sweater tighter around his aching shoulders, comforted by its pressure and warmth during this melancholy moment. Aaron paused and looked out at the crowd with concern. He saw that they were not just here to listen to the fate of Engineer Paulos, but to hear what they should do with their own lives, and what this episode meant for their own futures. The burden grew heavier, and Aaron pulled his sweater tighter, steadying himself, bracing for his delivery.

"As I was walking up here, I heard someone say, 'They never let him belong,' and I have to wonder about that. He had his papers, so he belonged in the eyes of the state. He was a citizen. He worked and contributed his skills, so he belonged in the eyes of the economy. But we can't forget the slights and hurts of these past months, and then ultimately what was done to him that made it seem clear that no matter how much good he did, he was unwanted by some in our town. But can we really let others define what it means to belong? For any of us? He chose to be here despite the escalating slurs and the escalating vandalism and the escalating confrontations. He stayed through all of that, and he had a life here he made a commitment to. And so I think that means he belonged here then and he belongs here now. I have to agree with my sister, Liya—wouldn't sending him back, albeit in his casket, just be a concession that intolerance has won?"

Aaron ended there, eager to walk his aching legs back to his seat and hoping that question would get time to hang in the air, but Mrs. Sarah quickly took her turn as she'd been waiting in the wings to have the final say—well, the penultimate say since Adam was slated for last. Still, she held considerable influence. If she sided with siblings Liya and Aaron, then the outcome would be decided: he'd stay. Otherwise, there'd be a tie that Adam, who presided over the occasion, would break. So the assembly leaned in as she made clear her views.

"I read in the news that after those men attacked him, they were spreading rumors that he was un-American, can you imagine? Engineer Paulos who would stop the car if he was listening to a game and the national anthem came on, then get out of the car to stand and put his hand on his heart. And who still played his Whitney Houston recording of the national anthem from time to time when he was feeling low down. Engineer Paulos who was in charge of our town's Fourth of July fireworks. Who read all those US history books. Engineer Paulos, who did his part, was called Un-American, can you imagine?

"If he was 'un' anything, it was unassuming, unhurried, unpretentious, unforgettable, and in the end, unfortunate. Engineer Paulos deserved so much more than what he got, and this town doesn't deserve to house his remains. It's unleashing these energies that are unlawful, unjust, unmoored, and it's unbefitting of him. Something is bringing forth a mean-hearted and mean-spirited force, nothing like the kind of loving town that drew us all in. They took his taxes, took his skills, took his best years, took his faith, took his life. Why should he lay down with them now and for eternity? He was a proud man. I am a proud woman. We are a proud community. They made him suffer. He was a proud man and should be able to go to where he can rest in respect."

Mrs. Sarah looked like she was about to crumple under the pressure of this task and paused until strength returned. Like she said, she was a proud woman. She shook Adam off when he went to comfort her and made a point of going back to her seat unassisted, unshaken, and undeterred.

And so Adam was left to deliver the final verdict, and he stood at the podium to address the somber room. He searched the anxious eyes of the men, women, and children in front of him, all looking up to him, and he felt the burden of his authority. He breathed in and said from deep within, "'They made him suffer,' we say. What 'they' are we talking about? Are we talking about our friends and neighbors who put signs in their yards saying immigrants are welcome and that they stand up for us? The ones who try to remind us of that in as many ways as they can? Are we talking about our colleagues and our kids' teachers? What 'they' are we afraid of? Fear is a powerful emotion. It's compelling—it compelled that mob to go after Engineer Paulos, and it's compelling us to question our rightful place here after that crime. But I hope that rationality can overcome their fear. We can't let a small few drive us to fear."

Adam paused as he grappled with the hollowness of what he'd just said. Not that it wasn't true, necessarily, but the rational reality was anyone at all could have committed this crime, he just didn't know. He didn't know who, he didn't know how many, he only knew why. And beyond this crime, what about all the anonymous and spiteful words that were a daily assault and had shattered the serenity of their lives? Who had scrawled slurs on the town's one billboard? Who were all those advocating for the ouster of immigrants on the comments in the local online news? Who owned the fake accounts that trolled their social media, spewing xenophobic insults unprovoked? And again, who attacked Engineer Paulos? What if it *was* their friends or neighbors who did it, the very ones who put signs in their yards saying immigrants are welcome? What if it *was* their colleagues or their kids' teachers, the very ones who smiled at them every day? Or someone else—the police chief, a doctor, a taxi driver? And regardless of who committed the crime, who knew about it, permitted it, allowed it to happen, protected the assailants, continued to protect them? Without attribution, the hate seemed everywhere. And so did the fear.

"I can understand," Adam continued, "given the circumstances of this crime, why we think this place isn't welcoming enough anymore, open enough, worthy enough a place for Engineer Paulos to find peace. Or worthy enough a place for any of us to find any peace, either. And this has made us ask ourselves if we can find stability and belonging here, too. If we ourselves should keep calling this our home. Even when we have our papers and we have made vows to this land, we know that only goes so far in making us feel embraced. But should we let the terror of this crime define what this town is? Should we let it restrict our lives within it? Can we find a way forward while staying right here? Can we believe in those who stand with us and can we have confidence that the futures we build here are genuine? Don't we know this to be true?"

Those before him waited for an answer to these very questions, and hearing them back didn't help them find the guidance they sought. He could see their frustration. He knew how personal and weighty this was, not just so they could resolve this matter for Engineer Paulos, but so they could find meaning for themselves, too. But who was he to answer any of this for them? How does anyone even begin to answer these questions? He'd lived eight decades, and all he knew was that it would be brave to leave; it would be brave to stay. It would take an act of massive courage to pack all their things in search of a new home; it would take an act of massive courage to shelter in place and have faith in the goodness that they knew could exist around them. It would require almost superhuman strength to pick up yet again and move on; it would require almost superhuman strength to decide that they would remain here despite obstacles yet to come. Who could say which was the right thing to do? Especially in that moment, Adam knew there were no right answers.

"I think we need to focus on what our departed friend would have wanted. Being the first in our community to be buried in this town, that would send a strong and subtle message, a message that we are settling down here as much as anyone, and Engineer Paulos liked to send a strong, subtle message. Maybe the best I can offer is to choose a path that allows him one more act of expression, one more stoic, silent statement to the world. And that does count for something. So for his sake, I am voting to lay Engineer Paulos down here, for he would want to dig in ever more firmly in these turbulent times. And for you all, stand steady against the harshness around us, and declare, with conviction, that here or away, you will find your home. Peace be with you."

There was a soft rustling—palms rubbed, backs patted, heads shaking, heads nodding, legs crossing and uncrossing. There was never going to be a perfect resolution here. Something would always feel unsettled, Adam knew this, but he also knew that, still, this imperfect determination was better than none at all. He looked out at uneasy faces and could feel that while the air had been cleared of one question, many others remained.

"We elders," Adam concluded, pointing at the others, Mrs. Sarah, Aaron and Liya, at Sesi, himself, "we thank you for being here as we confront this loss together as a community. The loss of Engineer Paulos was a terrible loss, but we won't let it steal everything away from us, not yet. No one took away our ability to be generous to friends and strangers and to give back to our town and to love and to heal and to imagine a better future. And as for how to move forward? Be kinder than before, and maybe that will help us bury this fear. Be stronger and more resilient than before and maybe that will help bury this anger. Be more giving than ever and maybe that will help bury this injustice." Adam wished he could be sure of this, and he felt weighted down by the burden of leadership in unfamiliar, uncertain times. He concluded in a whisper, "Let's see . . . final words. We have use of the synagogue again next Sunday. At that time, we'll be accepting funds for the burial plot and begin to lay the matter to rest. I sincerely appreciate you all for your time, and for giving Engineer Paulos a more noble ending."

The Drought That Drowned Us

Deborah Azmera drowned in the drought. Deborah Azmera's brothers, sisters, parents, cousins, aunts, uncles, nieces, nephews, friends, neighbors—a village of fifteen huts clustered along the receding border of the Rift Valley—drowned with her in the drought.

The village used to call itself the mushrooming branch, for the handful of circular huts that lined the path from the once-raging river to the old trading post like mushrooms on a log. The village chose names thoughtfully, carefully, since giving a name was like bestowing a destiny. They based the names they chose on some essence of identity distilled in every case; this was never rushed. Like many did in the region, the villagers gave names to big events that took on a life of their own. In other parts, immense, intensifying storms were named, but here, droughts were called things like "chatterbox who can't take a hint," since it just went on and on and wouldn't leave them be. Or "overbearing in-laws" who say they'll visit for a weekend but have already moved all the furniture around. Or "blistering sun blistering feet" for all the feet they walked on hot, dry soil for water.

Not only did they inspire names, but the droughts gave rise to desperate measures: to prayers, to pleading songs, to the sacrifice of two chickens and even a goat, to questions about what they had done to deserve this plight and how to make it stop. After all, they'd honored the earth just as they always had—blessed each harvest; gave thanks at each meal; fell in step with the rhythms they encountered. And still, the next drought came early, and no one was ready to name it. It came so much faster than anyone thought possible. It was true that as the years went on, the droughts kept appearing sooner and sooner, and they stayed too long. But when a drought fell upon them before the preceding one had fully abated, the villagers knew that some new force was with them now. A drought that arrived on the heels of a departing one was unheard of. Like day following day, night after night.

They might have called it "Taker of all our buried treasure." "Stealthy taker taking and taking." Maybe "the taker," or "for the taking."

But the naming would come later for they hadn't had a chance to store any food or water after the last drought—called "empty-handed guest with an empty stomach"—so they had to abandon their land, with nothing to eat and nothing to drink. They'd already appealed to the wisdom of their ancestors, the earth, the heavens, but none seemed to hear them. They lost faith in their voices, in their knowledge, in the very soil beneath their feet. What was left? They had to move. They had to pack their bags and just go.

South and east would have put them in the path of turbulent borders and conflicts that they didn't understand and didn't know how to weather. West or north, they thought, were the only options. They'd heard of great rivers to the north and roads that led to the vast lakes. North they went. Deborah thought, perhaps they should call the drought "invisible army in hot pursuit."

As the village left their homes behind, they decided it was time to call themselves something new as well. They chose "the people with seeds in their pockets," for they brought the seeds they'd saved from the last crop with them to plant in their new home. They passed fertile land that was fenced off from every angle, owned by foreign corporations growing crops for sale abroad. They saw no way in, so instead continued to follow the road north, starving amid this inaccessible abundance.

They were offered a ride by a man who pulled up next to them and said he'd be their protector, their guardian.

"Like Mikael," Deborah recalled, making the sign of a shield. "Mikael," Deborah whispered. "Will you give us—" and Deborah clutched her stomach with both hands.

He said he would give them more than they could ask for. They asked for water and something to eat. Mikael gave them water and meat, fruit, and blankets. Nothing left to believe in, not even in themselves, they rode with him in search of home.

None of the people with seeds in their pockets had ever held a pen and none of them had ever signed their names. Their names all came from a Bible, told in pictures, a book shared through generations gifted to them by the only visitor their village ever entertained. Their names came from that book, passed down by word of mouth, and the stories, too. When Deborah Azmera was told to put her name on a line at the bottom of a piece of paper, she drew a judge's gavel and a sheaf of wheat, for Deborah was always drawn with a gavel, and Azmera the harvest. Only afterward did she ask why Mikael wanted to see her name. Mikael didn't seem to hear. He just said he would take them to the lakes, to the other side, where there are never droughts to speak of. Deborah wondered if they should consider calling the drought "when the arid earth brought us to our bounty." The others told her they'd need to wait and see.

As they reached the shores, Deborah said, "This is no lake." Mikael asked how she could think such a thing. "A lake doesn't have waves like this," she said, remembering the small ones she'd seen in her childhood, before they dried up and became fields, then sandlots. She asked, "Is this the sea?"

"Nonsense," Mikael said. "The lake is constantly flooding, so its properties change. Water comes and goes."

She didn't know whether to believe him, but it seemed possible and who was she to argue? Deborah did wonder why Mikael led them to a stranger's boat and whispered in his ear, but who was she to argue about this, either? What voice did she have anymore? The stranger counted the fifty-two villagers stepping onto a long raft that was secured with twine around logs. He counted again as the villagers held each other to keep their balance. Mikael threw a tarp to Deborah, and told them to take cover.

"Aren't you coming with us?" someone asked.

"No," Mikael answered. "We have to go save others," he said.

"Who is we?" someone asked.

"You can't leave us behind," someone else said.

Others began to protest, too, that this wasn't right, but their voices didn't sway him, either. Mikael waved goodbye as Deborah and her village were drifting away on the choppy waters.

Their raft tossed and crashed against the waves. The people with seeds in their pockets did not cry, for they were afraid to waste their tears, to shed any water, for who knew when they'd be able to drink again. The villagers were afraid to sleep, for food was running out, and the helmsman would unceremoniously push a sleeping villager over the edge from time to time as their supplies dwindled. The waters were harsh, the land always seemed distant, ever out of reach, since none of the villagers knew how to swim. Why would they know, and how could they have learned? The villagers drowned like stones. When the raft finally approached the shore, only Deborah, along with the helmsman, remained on it—the people of her village in the grave of the waters behind her.

She heard the helmsman say they were nearing Aden, but as dawn softened the night, a police siren flashed and sounded, and the helmsman turned the raft right around. Deborah could see the helmsman make a calculation, look at the food in his bag, look at her frail body, look at the authorities on the shore. "No," she gasped, beating her fist into her open palm like crushing grains in a mortar as she used to do when they had a real yield, or as if she was pounding a gavel that represented her name, her being. "No, no," she gasped again, using her fist to argue for her life, striking this stranger's arms, his chest. But the sea didn't hear her.

In the moments before she was pushed, she thought, maybe we should call it "the drought that led us to the flood," or "the drought that drowned us all." As she felt the water enveloping her, Deborah tasted its salt, and imagined herself sinking into her village's tears. She touched the seeds in her pocket and scattered them around her, wondering if they could grow here, if all of their seeds would take root here. She wondered, when these waters receded, if they would leave behind rows and rows of harvest—a field here to be reaped, fertile plains to be populated, a legacy to pass down to the earth that bore them all these years.

A Down Home Meal
for These Difficult Times

The Riverside Church was like no house of worship Jazarah and Yeshi had ever seen. It had a gym, it had a view, it had a labyrinthine underbelly and an information desk that displayed notable moments like MLK Jr.'s famous speech about Vietnam delivered from its pulpit. And in one of the many community rooms in the basement, every Sunday there was a children's Amharic class to support the Ethiopian community that was trying to establish itself in makeshift ways in the American '80s. The immigrants attended early morning services at Greek, Russian, or Armenian Orthodox Churches, which were much closer to their own Ethiopian Orthodox tradition. The Eastern Europeans would stare at them huddled in the back pews, praying incomprehensible prayers, but otherwise seemingly at home with the dark hall and the low-toned chanting and the incense and the long service. Afterward, they'd make their way to the Riverside Amharic classes.

"Who could ever get anywhere this way," Jazarah said to Yeshi, who she met standing in the back of the classroom, watching their sleepy children struggling to learn the language of their ancestors, another concession made to life in America. Jazarah shook her head thinking of how she herself had moved through air thick with these words, breathed them in, let them course through her, then exhaled them in some innate, effortless way. "It's too hard for them to learn like this."

"They're children, they'll pick it up," Yeshi said, proud, in fact, to hear her language in such an esteemed establishment.

Yeshi and Jazarah talked about their experience as refugees, their assimilation, and all the fretful things they were learning to dread as they resettled in the States. Looming large was the PTA bake sale. They'd already just attended the PTA potluck, where, to their horror, everyone had to bring a dish to a party they'd been *invited* to. When the potluck was done, they watched in confusion as everyone took back their leftovers.

"It's like no one wants to be indebted to anyone else in this country," Jazarah said.

Yeshi added, "This is America, where everyone wants to be independent." They hated the idea of a bake sale almost as much as they hated the idea of a potluck almost as much as they hated to cook at all.

Yeshi was the first to confess that she was clueless in the kitchen. "Truth be told," she said, "I'm a terrible cook. I trained in the sciences, and I never had any taste for domestic duties back home."

It was a relief for Jazarah, who'd never felt guilty that she was a negligent homemaker until she came to the US. On account of being seriously rich back home, she had maids, cooks, housekeepers. She'd often gone weeks without stepping foot in the kitchen. Jazarah admitted, "As a cook, I'm catastrophic. I'd much rather window-shop, which must come as a surprise to some people. When I first got here, the man who met me at the Refugee Welcome Center in Albany was surprised to see I had shoes and a coat, even more so that they were leather. He told me, 'We didn't know Ethiopians had access to those.' The way he said it, it was like he meant clothes at all."

Yeshi asked, "Does your husband cook?"

Jazarah replied, "Never. Yours?"

"Wouldn't be caught dead in the general vicinity of a stove."

Yeshi asked, "Want to learn to cook?"

Jazarah said, "Not at all. You?"

Yeshi asked, "Is it a requirement?"

It did, though, seem like a requirement to them, somehow entangled in the American view of womanhood and femininity. They'd always been outliers of sorts, but they'd assumed coming to the US, they'd be able to completely reinvent their identities as women in a wholly liberated way. It didn't work out like that at all. In America, there were no extended families who were constantly inviting them over to eat, tending to maybe four, maybe five dinners a week. In America, there was no Aunt Adanech who would make weekend lunches while Yeshi tutored the kids in biology and geometry. There were no great-grands and cousins-thrice-removed to look after their kids when Jazarah had to catch up on work, and no doting neighbors to look in on the kids in the yard when Yeshi was having afternoon coffee with her husband. The pressure of their task as women, as mothers, as homemakers just seemed so much more burdensome here, and yes, somehow cooking every meal for just their small families felt like not only a waste of energy but also a national prerequisite.

As Yeshi and Jazarah stood in the church's classroom watching their kids go through the Amharic alphabet and mispronounce their own names, they decided they'd make something together for the upcoming bake sale, combining forces the way they would have back in old days.

* * *

Finding the quintessential American cookbook for the quintessential American woman was a task they took on with relish—as if the dishes held some secret to their new identities—and they sought out just the perfect combination of recipes for all their new obligations. They walked into a bookstore by the Riverside Church when the kids were getting their weekly lessons, and they hadn't expected to find so many options in the separate section that was reserved just for the genre.

"What I wouldn't give to have my grandmother's recipes written down, just to see them," Yeshi said.

"My grandmother claimed she was allergic to the kitchen, and she'd start sneezing anytime she approached it," Jazara replied. "She was also allergic to the broom closet and the washbasin."

"My kind of woman," Yeshi said.

A sales associate walked over, lingered near Yeshi and Jazarah so as not to interrupt but also to make it clear that she was there to help. Jazarah spoke up, "Miss, oh miss. What is the most American of these?"

"I mean, American food is just food," the clerk replied, walking over with her hands folded across her chest.

"Of course all food is food," Yeshi agreed.

The clerk laughed a little, and said, "But American food isn't really a thing. It's like a melting pot of things. It's everything and it's nothing."

"What we mean is, we need a good, popular, pleasing American cookbook," Jazarah clarified.

"This is our bestseller," the clerk said holding up *The Good Housekeeping Illustrated Cookbook*, adding, "it's an instant classic with each new edition."

"It has a certain ring to it," Jazarah said, taking the book from the clerk.

"Doesn't it?" Yeshi agreed. "Who doesn't want to keep their house?"

"I've lost two already—one to the Derg in 1975, one to the Derg in 1979—so I'd love to keep mine as long and as good as I can," Jazarah mused.

"I've lost three already—one to the floods, one to the Derg, one to the counterrevolution—so I couldn't agree more," Yeshi said.

"This series is your best bet, then. They go way back," the clerk said, showing them a ratty, tattered early edition. She opened it to the front, and Yeshi read, "Good Housekeeping for the Advancement of the American Home."

"That sounds important," noted Jazarah.

"And they have a department of household engineering," Yeshi said.

"I like that, too," Jazarah said. "Authoritative. This book is an authority."

"It's right up my alley, the science and mathematics of trying to keep one's home," Yeshi emphasized. "A pretty complicated equation, I know from experience."

They were sold. Yeshi and Jazarah picked out the least expensive edition they could find. As the clerk rang up their order, she said, "Don't start with this recipe," pointing to an image of a soufflé.

"Maybe you should start with an omelet. Like a Denver omelet is a very American omelet."

"What else?" they asked.

"Lasagna is good. That's a favorite of mine for dinner parties and potlucks."

"Oh good, what else?" They were getting excited.

"Oh I don't like meatloaf, but it's common. And fried rice is a crowd-pleaser. And tater tots."

"Tater tots, tater tots. Good, good. What else?" They were almost ecstatic now.

"There are a lot of diagrams in the book," the clerk said. "So it's okay if you don't know English very well."

Jazarah and Yeshi didn't respond to that snub disguised as a helpful footnote. They walked off, flipping through the glossy photos in the front section where dishes seemed shellacked, thoughtfully lit, and posed, almost.

Indeed, they did not start with soufflé, but they also didn't start with the omelet. While Richard Simmons was bouncing on the TV yelling at them to "lift, lift, turn it, rumble, round the world," they were baking a pineapple upside-down cake that they thought was the most fitting of all their options, a reflection of how everything had flipped around, their lives, their identities, and here they were baking a mixed-up dessert to raise funds for a gymnastics meet in Schenectady.

* * *

Every time there was a big upset in their lives, big enough a shock to rock foundations, pull at rugs underfoot, threaten to take yet another home away from them, Yeshi and Jazarah made a dish from *The Good Housekeeping Illustrated Cookbook* as a sort of superstitious offering to the Gods of the Department of Household Engineering, praying that they got to keep what they had, even if they had to promise to strive for no more. In their shaky times, they picked recipes at random or with intention, and made them over and over until they had been perfected. They'd go to Yeshi's home in Sunset Park or Jazarah's home in the Rockaways not so much to cook but to pay homage to this most sacred and difficult task of staying put.

When Yeshi's husband lost his job, they made Classic Chili con Carne four times. They went to the Goodwill to buy kitchen equipment, then hid it from their husbands, who would rather have one new pot and one new spatula than bags of things that had been owned by who-knew-who and given away for who-knew-why. Yeshi carefully leveled the ingredients in a measuring cup like she was in her old chem lab. Jazarah chatted as she burned the garlic and overcooked the meat. They both thought it needed a few extra dashes of chili powder, and both hailed the inclusion of sugar, marveled over the Worcestershire sauce and decorative parsley. Yeshi triumphantly finished the dish with grated cheddar and sour cream. Before they took their first bites, they said a few words to the spirit of good housekeeping: "May Yeshi's home remain prosperous though her husband is out a paycheck, and may work quickly flow back in the way it left."

Which it did, until Yeshi's husband lost his next job, and they made batches of Emergency Corn Biscuits.

When Yeshi's husband left her for a blonde waitress, they made Broiled Hamburg Steak, just the once.

When Yeshi's husband came crawling back and she had to

change the locks, they made Scalloped Ham and Potatoes for a week.

When Jazarah had to suspend her education to pay for the car repair, they made Mashed Yams and Buttered Beets for lunch and dinner.

When Jazarah's daughter was hospitalized with a severe case of pneumonia, they made the perfect Apple Pandowdy.

When Jazarah's credit cards were stolen and maxed out, they made trays of Corn Fritters.

Once a month, they made a Beef Stew for the kitchen of the Riverside Church.

In the weeks after 9/11, they made every recipe in the dessert section, and wearing American flag pins, brought coolers to the relief workers stationed at the piers off the West Side Highway, where the rescue mission gathered: the Mayor's Office, the Red Cross, the firefighters, the police, the computer engineers who worked on logistical software. The street in front of the pier was lined with garbage trucks supposedly to dissuade car bombers, and the river behind the pier was lined with barges to supposedly prevent boat bombers. The fences outside the pier were covered with photographs of missing loved ones. People milled around the pictures desperately seeking answers or silently holding vigil. Yeshi and Jazarah stood there among them every evening, and for the first time since they came to the US, they shared their own stories with strangers, revealing that they had escaped a brutal dictatorship, that some in their families had also gone missing, and that the hope for their return never really goes away. They camped out with their Ziploc bags full of sweets and chatted with exhausted relief workers coming or going. A few times, Yeshi and Jazarah were even invited to watch the game at a nearby bar on those warm fall evenings in New York as the Yankees made their way well into the postseason.

After the recession in 2008, Yeshi and Jazarah got back to cooking in a fit. Their copy of *The Good Housekeeping Illustrated Cookbook* was never more needed, the magic they attributed to it never more urgent. They chose to focus on perfecting the "economy holiday foods," not to celebrate of course, but to comfort. They brought plates to their neighbors who were being evicted. As often as they could, they brought whole chickens to the Riverside Church for those in need. They cooked for themselves, too, when they both lost their jobs as receptionists after their companies folded, and they scrambled to figure out what to do next. Their kids were grown and gone, so Jazarah and her husband moved into Yeshi's cheaper and smaller home as they all tried to make ends meet.

In 2009, still having no steady work for over a year, and having gone backward and forward through that cookbook, Yeshi and Jazarah took the last of their savings and bought an old van that didn't run, towed it next to a parking lot up by the Riverside Church, and opened a stationary food truck selling "A Down Home Meal for These Difficult Times." There was only one item on the menu, "the Sack Lunch," and whatever recipes they made that day went inside. One of their regular customers—a construction worker—said it was like being a kid and opening his lunchbox on the playground, while a yogi said it gave her a chance to practice the act of receiving with grace, though a Harlem hipster blogged that the best part was the "authentic, unpretentious approach." When they handed their customers their brown paper bags, Yeshi and Jazarah would point at the sign and say what customers took to be an imperative, a wish, their blessing, "a *down home* meal to keep your home good and tied down," which patrons found endearing. They crafted a small seating area just to the side of the truck, and in streamed the cabbies taking breaks from their shifts, and the Columbia students shuttling to and fro, and the store owners heading over to their shops on Broadway, and the commuters coming in from the GW Bridge, and the congregants and the priests and the park-goers and eventually businesspeople, too. More tables had to be brought in, of course, more folding chairs, and one patron said it was starting to look like Bryant Park over there, which they took for a compliment. The lines grew long and began to form before they opened. One day a famous chef with an Ethiopian background even came by and told them it was "great work."

And at that moment, what had been this hobby—this habit, this salvation, not even a passion, but a custom they very much came to need—had become their work. They started to see that what comforted them comforted those around them, too. What fed them fed others. What grounded them seemed to hold down their customers, who said that a meal at "Down Home" was like being at the timeless American family table, everyone from everywhere coming together to press pause on their long days, sharing the same food: one plate, one fate.

The whimsical menus became more planned and plotted, and the care that went into choosing the items each week was the care that went into reading bedtime stories to their kids with the most authentic American accents they could manage decades ago or sewing the best red, white, and blue dresses they could afford for their immigration interviews years before that or strategizing every detail of their routes West even before that. They thought everyone should start the week with a hearty meal, so Mondays' choices were heavier: more protein, more carbs, sometimes fried pork, sometimes biscuits and beans. By Thursdays, the menu was playfully anticipating the weekend, a peek-a-boo chicken and Celebration Layer Cake. Saturdays were all about the aroma and warmth of home: cinnamon pastries, ham and bacon, roasting coffee, fries, fresh fruit, stove-grilled meats. They took Sundays off.

The care that went into redecorating the eating area was the care that went into buying the best red, white, and blue dresses they could afford for their citizenship swearing-in ceremonies, and years later, of personally inviting each of their neighbors to their kids' graduations, and years after that, personally inviting those same neighbors to their children's weddings, like in the old days, rounding up the whole village to celebrate together. For the seating, Yeshi and Jazarah chose sturdy chairs that were anchored to the floor with chains and tent pins. They hand-painted flowers on the tabletops that always looked fresh.

They printed out hundreds of fliers and tucked them under the windshields of the cars parked in the commuter lot, passed them out at the Little League games down the block, delivered them door to door. They were able to hire staff, start second careers, rotate in and out of this life that began to run all on its own. Their grown children had anniversary parties at the food truck lot. Their grandkids had christenings and birthday parties there. Friends and neighbors would stop in for old-style American lunches and to catch up with each other on sunny afternoons. Sometimes chic urbanites and out-of-towners came by holding reviews published in off-the-beaten-path travel guides touting this well worthwhile tucked-away spot that takes forever to find but that makes you feel like you've finally landed. When the pandemic descended and restaurants around the city closed, their lines got longer, the accessibility appreciated, and the need for comfort and connection even stronger.

It took all the effort in the world, but it happened quite organically nonetheless that the little vehicle of a truck had sunk several inches and settled into the plot of earth it occupied, had established itself and them in the city, had supported their lives, had given them purpose, community, deliverance, too. One day after a long, fruitful week, someone suggested they fix up that old van and get it to run, bring their Down Home dining to Wall Street or Williamsburg, where they'd make a killing, but Yeshi and Jazarah couldn't even comprehend why—why should all of the energy they'd spent to stay in one place be cast aside so lightly? No, for as long as they could, they'd continue on right there in that stationed van with moss on its wheels, a palm-sized sparrow's nest under its front bumper, vines growing up its façade and around the spokes of the hubcaps, a webbing of roots. The fingers of roots curled around their lives, too, sprouting from seeds they never meant to plant, never consciously watered, but that had taken hold anyway because life adapts, or tries. These roots that cradled their lives were ripped away from time to time, trampled, shook loose, but slowly, slowly pushed through, steadied them as Yeshi and Jazarah stood ever more firmly on ground that had to be home.

Preludes

1. Moving Day

According to the local bloggers, the latest census identified 98118, the Rainier Valley in South Seattle, as the most diverse zip code in the US. This happened over time, first the American Indians, then the white settlers, Black migrants from Southern states, immigrants from China, Vietnam, Korea, the Philippines, and most recently, from around the Horn of Africa. The diversity was not accidental, since North side properties once had clauses like: *No person of Asiatic, African, or Negro blood, lineage or extraction shall be permitted to occupy said property.* Amare lived south of that red line. When he'd bought a home four years earlier with a down payment he'd saved up from working back-to-back shifts at a gas station, he felt he'd finally become a real American, more so than when he got his green card, his citizenship, his English proficiency certificate, his driver's license, his Ford. He owned an unmovable, solid little plot of his new country, and that mattered. The American flag he hung the day he signed the mortgage was still waving from the porch the day he was set to leave.

The cottonwood trees near Lake Washington were already shedding their small fluffy seeds, the mid-spring winds carried the silky white fibers in the air like a blizzard blowing through the neighborhood. Amare watched his six-year-old son, Yonathan, catching shiny clusters, pinching the captured seeds, then releasing, resting them on the backs of the breeze. The block was quiet; his neighbors had long ago taken down their HOPE '08 lawn signs, and many had since traded them for SALE signs. Some had already abandoned their homes, and long grass and overgrown hedges trapped the white cottonwood fluff in tangles of dead leaves and twisted branches.

Amare stood in the shade of a eucalyptus, now at least fifteen feet tall and gaining strength. It had risen quickly, soundlessly, had grown without Amare much noticing, a transformation like vapor from the Puget Sound over the Juan de Fuca Strait, like the great silent surge of a sparrow's wings unfolding. He feared that he had somehow fallen outside the grace of that lifting force, the elevating promise of the country he tried to make his own. Amare struggled to hold on to the thought that neither had abandoned him, neither had given up on him, not really, even if he hadn't known that feeling for years, ever since he lost his grounding, his wife got sick, her insurance was terminated, he had to balance child-rearing/work/caregiving, his bank offered a second mortgage that had something called an adjustable arm, and the interest hiked, and the debt piled on, and he lost his wife as he spent the better part of two years on the brink of ruin until one day ruin came.

Amare swept fallen eucalyptus leaves from the porch. He moved the broom along the porch frame breaking up spiderwebs. He used his thumbnail and index finger to clip off a few dry leaves from the planters by the front door, then tucked his thumb into his shirtsleeve to polish the bronze-plated numbers on the door, 374.

Someone called his name, and Amare turned to see Marla Mason walking her cat, wearing her practical shoes and covered head to toe in a colorful hijab and dress. Born in the Caribbean and raised in the Rainier Valley, Marla was what could be called a "porous" personality. She took on the qualities of her ever-changing neighborhood as if her skin were no barrier, but instead an open door. A woman of many conversions, Marla had most recently started dressing differently, an act of apparent liberation for her but a source of total discomfort for her husband, who feared what people might think it said about *him* ("But I want you to feel free," and she had said, "I am," to which he had said, "But others might get the impression that—" but by then Marla was out the door, carrying her pet, Eco, in one arm and dialing numbers on her cell with the other, setting out to make the rounds).

"Now, Amare, sit down," Marla said, bringing Eco onto her lap. "You've been working on this house so much it's like you're trying to sell it all over again." She patted the step, but he kept cleaning.

"I just want to leave this property as nice as when I got it."

"I hope you don't feel guilty for losing your house," Marla whispered, leaning close.

Amare shrugged because of course he felt terribly guilty even though he had done every last thing he could think to do. He ended up with only stacks of documents for his troubles, including the diagram he tried to piece together of who exactly held his mortgage, which had so many lines moving in so many directions it looked like a plate of spaghetti. He used to think the act of acquisition was the most difficult thing—finding a wife and getting her to marry him, or finding a good home and putting something down—but these years taught him that holding on to what one got was the harder task.

"Where will you go?" Marla asked, and Amare knew enough to avoid her perceptive gaze. "You have no family. You'll break my heart if you tell me you're taking Yonathan to one of those tent towns."

Amare knocked on the wooden steps. "I got some help from the community and our church," he assured her.

"As long as you have some help, that's all I want to know," Marla said, but before she could ask the question forming on her lips, she was interrupted by Tariq, who was walking toward #374 wearing his kofia, long white linen shirt, white linen pants, hands held up high to the sky, praising the good Lord in every form, wherever he went, whenever he could.

"Good morning and assalamu alaykum," Tariq called out.

"Wa alaykum assalam," Marla replied.

"Good morning," Amare said.

"You going today, Amare?" Tariq asked. He took a step toward them, his shirt straightening out.

"Yes he is," Marla confirmed.

Tariq said to Amare, "This is turning into a quieter block now. Who's Marla gonna check in on with that cat of hers and gossip about once everyone leaves?"

"Tariq, I could spout about you all day every day and the well would never run dry," Marla shouted back.

"Whoa, I take it back. Not gonna put myself in your line of fire," Tariq said, adjusting his gravity-immune arms, knowing Marla could draw some heavy ammunition. "Amare, the universe provides, and so do good neighbors. Do you need anything?" Tariq asked.

Amare pursed his lips, for few things were as uncomfortable

to Amare as people going out of their way on his behalf, and he wondered if he had been a different man in that respect, then what else might be different. Everything, maybe. "I'm good," was all Amare said.

"Okay then," Tariq shouted. "Can't stay. The 42 bus is running late today, got me off schedule. May the dear Lord spare you from knowing any more trouble, may you be free of the trouble you've known," Tariq said as he walked away with his hands lifted to the sky, his chin turned up, basking in the heavenly glow that seemed to touch him and him alone on the street that morning.

Marla left to walk Eco down the road, peeking into open doors and open windows, and Amare went back to cleaning the house, until, looking at its fresh paint and polish, its swept-clean exterior and interior, its trimmed lawn, its manicured hedges, he decided he was ready.

2. The Floating House

Gashe Ayeloo and Eteye Amsala's house, #372, was next door to Amare's. Gashe Ayeloo's favorite way to waste a little time was to look out his window at people waiting for the bus; after all, his home had an ideal view of this little cul-de-sac branching off MLK. The house was three stories high and so old it seemed about to fall down, but instead it fell up, floating above the street below. Raised just slightly off the ground, quite literally levitating there. The exact height was two inches, according to Gashe Ayeloo. A small amount, but notable nonetheless.

Eteye Amsala was the first to notice. When she was on her way to her car one morning years back just after they moved in, she tripped. Looking around, she didn't see anything that would have made her stumble. Not a stone, not a root, not a stick in sight. But she saw a shadow that had not a leafy perimeter, but a root-rimmed one. Eteye Amsala ran back inside, and summoned her husband.

Gashe Ayeloo observed the miracle by leaning over the edge of his property, which he rarely left. Nothing seemed to be holding the house up. He looked overhead, but the answer was not in the sky, either. I thought I'd seen it all by now, he thought, though he wasn't quite sure what he was seeing. A small crowd began to gather. Yonathan, Amare's son, got a bag of marbles, rolled one under the house, then ran to the back, and returned holding up that marble, which had gone straight through. At this, the crowd shifted from a position of doubt to one of belief.

By this time, Eteye Amsala was hysterical. She swore up and down and left and right and side to side that she'd never step foot in that cursed abode. She went to church morning, noon, and night, and stayed with her cousin until Gashe Ayeloo protested her absence by fasting. The hunger strike lasted two days, and Eteye Amsala was guilted into coming home, but she couldn't help but creep softly through the house for fear that she might fall straight down and to who knew where. Eteye Amsala took another pre-caution: each morning, she'd open the gate and look outside just to make sure they hadn't finally drifted off to who knew where, either, for confronted with a mystery as peculiar as this, her imag-ination took flight, understandably.

Gashe Ayeloo's hovering house was a gossiped-about sight on this slice of the Rainier Valley . . . for a while. Some who were scientifically inclined thought about conducting experiments. The romantics dreamed this rebellious house was a symbol of wild nature. The bureaucratic wondered whether Gashe Ayeloo should pay more in property taxes since he technically occupied the land around and below his house. The superstitious had their own beliefs and crossed over to the other side of the street as they walked up and down that stretch of road. But as these things go, people got on tending to their own lives in this closed-off, separate corner of what was becoming known as Little East Africa, where signs in languages from around the Horn were juxtaposed over signs in Mandarin and Vietnamese, which were layered over signs in characters too faded to make out. The spectacle of Gashe Ayeloo's house also faded away, was absorbed and accepted as a neighborhood quirk soon enough.

Gashe Ayeloo accepted it, too, but had to take some practical measures to adapt (he said the pavers shifted on his doorstep more often than was reasonable, and swore more bugs, squirrels, and birds gravitated to his levitating parcel, and they needed shooing away), though he was surprised that the change required very little in the way of maintenance. Otherwise, there was nothing Gashe Ayeloo could seem to do to physically get that house back down, for the mechanism that kept his home suspended was not magic, not science, not an alternate dimension breaking through on this very spot, but a force that bubbled up from the will and internal desire of Gashe Ayeloo, who had set out to never leave Ethiopia, even long after he had gone, long after he'd been cast into exile. In his exile, he recreated his home off MLK Ave. to precisely mirror the first. This reflected house, like his life in the city, and his world itself, did not quite touch down, was neither here nor there.

Gashe Ayeloo's house wasn't the only home afloat in this world. There were probably dozens across the city, maybe hundreds across the country, perhaps even thousands across the globe, maybe many more. In fact, if you could look at the world from the side with exacting detail, from a hovering magnifying lens or some such gadget, you'd notice a strange topography of floating houses rising just above the earth, a separate plane of existence right there for anyone to see, should they choose to look. I know this for a fact and can assure you with confidence, for you see, I lived in one such house far from Gashe Ayeloo nearly a century ago and am no stranger to these shifts. I can say from experience that he is not alone. These floating homes constitute not any certain state, not a nation, not a formal country with any government or ideology or agencies that require paperwork and official stamps of entry. This is not a governed state, not even a state of mind, but a state of heart. A certain way of living in diaspora, and dear Gashe Ayeloo was not alone.

With homes like this, there are always those days when the foundation creaks a little, poised to touch down again and re-solidify, rejoin a fuller way of life. When I see Gashe Ayeloo, it makes me wonder, what does it take for a man like this to consider reengaging? For me, everything had to fall apart, and a new life, wholly unexpected, sprung up in its place. For Gashe Ayeloo, how great a force would be needed to nudge him those last two inches homeward?

In the meantime, he spent his days looking out from his window. That morning, as white cottonwood fibers blew through the air, Gashe Ayeloo waved to Tariq whose arms were raised tall and poised, recalling an old, rooted Mediterranean Cyprus, or a rocket set to lift off.

3. Shift Change

Across the street from Gashe Ayeloo's floating house stood a small apartment complex called Elysian Estates. The one-story structure had been built in the '70s, and from the street, each unit looked identical. The apartments were lined up in a row with their doors facing the street, A, B, C, D. Apartment A was occupied by Samson the jeweler and his two kids; apartment B belonged to Marla the busybody, her anxious husband, and her docile cat; Hannah the philosopher lived in apartment C with her books; apartment D was occupied by Elsie, Hirwi, and Mamush, cousins.

Hirwi and Mamush, who had been mathematicians back home, now drove a taxi they shared. It was 11:00 a.m., and Hirwi had just returned from driving his shift. Every day, Mamush would go out at 11:30 a.m. to drive the day shift until 11:00 p.m., then Hirwi would take the cab out again at 11:30 p.m. until 11:00 a.m. They spent these half hours together for meals at 11:00 a.m. and 11:00 p.m. each day. They had a one-bedroom apartment at Elysian Estates, and Hirwi and Mamush shared the bed, since neither slept when the other did. Elsie, a student, lived with them, too. She slept on the couch.

Hirwi walked in and shook off the cottonwood fibers that clung to his coat. The three cousins washed their hands, prayed, then ate together off the same plate. As they ate, they watched the midday news, which aired a report on the earthquake and tsunami that had hit Japan and caused the earth's axis to shift by four degrees, the earth's geography to readjust, the nuclear reactor to melt down. The footage on the screen showed nuclear administrators apologizing to the government and the people. The administrators acknowledged that they'd made a mistake, and then, wearing suits and polished shoes, flung themselves forth, prostrating themselves in front of the elected officials, begging the people for forgiveness. Elsie, Hirwi, and Mamush were moved.

Elsie, who had grown up in the US, said, "In America, an accusation is always followed by a defense. Who would just let themselves be accused and submit, begging like this? Anyone who does this deserves forgiveness."

Hirwi, famished from his long shift, chewed loudly as he spoke.

"But Elsie, you have not experienced what we have experienced. Mamush and I lived through a revolution and a dictatorship. Forgiveness for you will be something else altogether than forgiveness for me. These men's actions forced people to readjust their livelihoods, not to mention lose everything. Maybe their people will not forgive them. There are people in my life I can never forgive."

Mamush took a sip of water and thought about this before speaking. "But these scientists, when something went seriously wrong, they tried. I think if you try in good faith, then you can be forgiven. But as for me, there are also people I can never forgive."

"Think of Mengistu, the dictator during the Derg," Hirwi said, adding this descriptor for the benefit of Elsie, who'd been born in 1992, after the fall of the dictatorship. He stared quizzically at her.

"Mengistu? I know who he is," Elsie asserted. "My parents told me all about him, and I've done my homework, too."

"So you know he lives in a mansion in Zimbabwe?" Hirwi asked, then glared at Elsie.

"Yes, I do."

"And who is the leader who gave him protection?" Hirwi asked.

"Mugabe," Elsie said, as if she were being asked to add one and one.

"Did you know Mengistu was tried and convicted in absentia?" Mamush asked. "But never imprisoned?"

"Yes, I know," Elsie said as if she were being told the sun rises in the east.

"And that he justifies his actions to this day?" Hirwi jumped in.

"I know that, too," Elsie said, as if he'd said that Scheherazade was a gifted storyteller.

"And that he has left a population feeling homeless in the world?" Mamush continued.

"Of course," Elsie replied, as if he were revealing the restlessness in her heart.

"Mengistu should have asked for forgiveness, not expected exoneration," Mamush said.

"Would you have forgiven him then?" Elsie asked. She watched Hirwi wave away the question.

"I would not, but it would have made a difference," Mamush said.

"How?" Elsie asked.

"I don't know exactly," Mamush muttered.

Hirwi swallowed, then said, "It would have meant something to me, too. It would have mattered. I left my home to flee that man, his ruthless law, his tyrannical rule. He turned my home, our home, into a prison." Hirwi wiped his mouth, then flicked his napkin in the air as if he were directing traffic. He said loudly, "It would have mattered to know that the events that affected me affected him, the events that still haunt me still haunt him. I might have forgiven him then."

"But some people don't feel remorse," Elsie noted.

Hirwi put his napkin back on his lap. "Why should I accept that?"

Mamush mused, "Enough about the past. We should look ahead and live as if we throw ourselves at the feet of life asking for its blessing."

"So why don't you?" Elsie asked.

"Some of us do," Mamush said. "Many really do." Mamush paused, then added, "But on the other hand, some think they are owed."

"I think I am owed," Hirwi said.

"Owed what?" Elsie asked.

"That," Hirwi said, pointing at the television showing the repentant men still bowing down.

Hirwi took out his satchel and started adding up his earnings from his shift. "The bus was slow again, slower than usual, so I picked up a lot of fares on the way," Hirwi said and handed Mamush the empty satchel, then gave Elsie twenty dollars.

"What for?" Elsie asked.

"A rainy day, kid," Hirwi said.

"This is Seattle, so that won't be long," Mamush said, but no one laughed. Elsie thanked Hirwi and settled in front of the computer, and Hirwi and Mamush read over her shoulder as she scrolled through the online diaspora news outlets to learn something of home.

4. The Newcomer

The time difference between Addis Ababa and Seattle is ten hours in the spring. A typical flight from Bole International to SEA/TAC might stop over in Khartoum, refuel in Rome, there would be a transfer in DC, and one final leg to Washington State, a total of twenty hours without delays. But a trip like this felt even longer because of idling in airports, lingering in the duty-free, frantically retrieving luggage, going through customs, rechecking bags. In other words, even though from Seattle, Addis Ababa was half a world away, ask anyone, it felt as far as another one altogether.

Aida had not been back to Addis in decades, and it had been that long since she'd last seen her brother. He was a writer, and though she used to read his work, he'd recently stopped writing altogether, and she'd heard nothing from him until that short letter only saying, "Can you send me a plane ticket? Quickly? Please." And her even shorter reply, "Enclosed."

Aida's duplex was brand new, part of a large lot of identical homes reserved for low-income families that occupied the corner between the floating house and MLK Ave. Aida's lawn was lush, full of cottonwood flurries that clung to the blades, but despite this, the landscaping felt sterile: so much green, so little life.

Aida looked at her watch. It was night in Addis, 9:15 p.m. Mateos would be ready to go to the airport. The air in Addis would be foggy and cool, the scent of the eucalyptus already fading. Aida sat in a quiet corner in the kitchen and redialed the number for the fifth time. She was determined to say hello, to see if her brother would need anything, to ask how he was feeling, to know it was really happening. She was ready with her prepaid phone card, coffee brewed. Her husband already at work, Aida sat alone and entered the number. The automated voice, saccharine, staccato, asked for her pin. You have . . . thirty . . . minutes remaining. Aida rolled her eyes. She had wasted as much time just trying to get through and would have to buy another card if she used this one up, and by then it might be too late to call.

All she got was a busy signal, the network still jammed. She would call back later. Killing time, she decided to inspect the basement, smoothed the comforter on what would soon be Mateos's bed, tidied up her brother's new space again. She had gone back and forth about the things to buy, saving, purchasing, returning, exchanging until she had at least a little something in the room that would make her brother at ease. A few books. A spare chair with extra blankets, a couple of plants. Aida often walked through the rooms and pictured what her brother might do there. What he might want, need. She imagined his presence, and the way that he would occupy the space, bring some energy to it, and put it to use.

Before, the walls had been bare but now were adorned with two posters from Goodwill, a close-up of a Monet lily, and a single frantic sunflower by Van Gogh. There were family photos, too, some originals, some scanned and printed, all lacked luster, something having faded with age or in the transfer. She felt a strange impulse to study these photos to be sure she remembered her brother's face. Funny things happen to memory over time, everyone knew that. What should never be forgotten can be lost, and all the wrong things can persist. She worried that she would walk through the airport, passing her brother like a stranger. She examined a photo focusing on the heart-shaped birthmark over his eye (left, she confirmed), his crooked front tooth (left, too). Then she wondered, if she had changed as much as she felt she had, would her brother recognize her?

She thought of her own flight out of the country and how nervous she had been, not of flying, but of landing, and she wondered how her brother was feeling, if he was sick with nerves or just exhausted. Had he been tending to final obligations, parting promises, rounds of goodbyes, rushed favors, or would he, like her, just slip away?

Aida went back to her desk. Only five minutes had gone by since she last tried to call her brother. She put a CD in her computer and began listening to a tizita, the music of homesickness, humming along to a recording that sounded scratchy and distant, and always had. For Aida, nostalgia was built on a vague melancholy for a life cut short, a life that came unraveled before it could start. That stolen life used to mean growing up in one neighborhood, going to the local school, spending weekends with a family that extended as far along a tree as the old aunties could trace, meeting a man and adding to that sprawling orchard, getting old, watching the next generation take over. That's what she had to give up to be here, and she knew that, but now her brother was coming to her, and she wondered if some part of her former self would return with him, and how much of that self she actually still longed for.

When the tizita ended, the song on repeat started over. Aida imagined a record player, the arm picking itself up and moving back to the beginning without skipping a beat or scratching on the grooves, and then she pictured that she herself held the song somewhere inside herself, that something within her was circling round and round, then being pulled back again.

As she listened to the music, Aida dragged her cursor across the Google Maps screen, zoomed in on the satellite image, the arrow hovering over her brother's house, her childhood home. She wished she could see inside. The neighborhood looked completely different again, construction cones dotted the street, scaffolding made of uneven tree trunks held up buildings-in-progress, looking like pins jutting out from square pin cushions. Aida clicked the arrows north, south, east, and west to tour that slant of land where she had been raised. She guided the arrow of her mouse north, the view on the screen moving up the hillside, up to the peaks that looked out over the city as she redialed the number and tried again.

5. Arrivals

By now, a crowd was anxiously awaiting the 42 bus, pacing, peeking in on neighbors, starting up one random conversation after the next, dropping stories halfway to listen to gossip, spread gossip. Amare and Yonathan stood at the bus stop next to two big suitcases with Marla Mason there next to them, and Tariq, too, with his back arched and arms up high. Aida had stopped by to chat with Elsie, who used a magazine to shield her eyes from the floating lustrous cottonwood seeds, which glowed in the air like iridescent feathers.

Mamush drove the cab out of his driveway and idled in front of the bus stop. "Amare," he called out. "Where are you going?"

"Downtown," Amare said, gesturing with his head toward the cluster of high-rises that could be seen in the distance to the north, opposite the peak of Mt. Rainer to the south.

"Can I give you a lift?" Mamush asked. "It would be my pleasure."

Amare hesitated, and Mamush added, "No problem for me. It'll be easier to pick up a fare downtown." To that, Amare agreed.

As Mamush opened his trunk, and as Amare and Yonathan pulled their bags to the cab, a large U-Haul drove by the bus stop and toward #374.

On the side of the U-Haul was a picture of a woman standing in front of a pueblo and what looked like the Grand Canyon. They watched the slow truck park in front of #374 and looked on curiously as a man stepped out of the truck and waited in front of the house.

"Where's he from?" Mamush asked Amare.

Everyone was silent, curious, tense, awkwardly watching the stranger arrive on their block. Aida looked around at the cold reception the neighbors were offering and said, "Someone should go talk to him, welcome him." And someone would have, but a shadow came up behind the crowd, and they turned to see an even bigger truck had rounded the corner off MLK and sluggishly zigzagged onto their street. The truck had its wipers on slow, rhythmically clearing cottonwood from the gigantic windshield of this barge of a vehicle.

"Isn't that a . . . look at that, what's on the back of that truck?" asked Marla.

"Is that a house?" Tariq called out, pumping his raised arms.

The crowd could just make out the outline of a large, two-story home.

"They're like turtles, these people," said Marla. "Where do they come from?"

The house had beige aluminum siding and a red roof. The windows had white lace curtains, frames painted bright red. This home was cared for. In fact, it looked brand new.

"Are they going to knock down my house?" Amare yelled.

Gashe Ayeloo threw open his window and poked his head way out. "Another floating house!" he exclaimed, but few paid attention to him.

"Hey," Tariq called out to the driver when the towed house inched by the bus stop. "What're you doing with that thing?"

"Welcome to our block," Aida said sweetly, and she looked around her, encouraging her neighbors to join her.

"Good morning!" the driver said obligingly, then rolled down the window to wave.

"What're you doing?" Tariq asked again, his hands now straight up in the air.

"My brother's moving to 374," he pointed to the man with the U-Haul waiting down the block, "and we figure there's enough land on that lot for two houses, so I'm bringing my family, too."

"How nice!" Aida said right away. For the others, the information took time to sink in, and Elsie slowly nodded, then Mamush, then Tariq, then Marla. Gashe Ayeloo looked at the lot next door to his as if imagining whether he could learn something from his new neighbors and their nimble home.

"Why didn't I think of that?" Amare mumbled. "Renting out part of the lot?"

"What? What would you have done?" asked Marla. "No, honey, you did everything you could, and now you need to move on."

The driver waved again and continued to steer the wide home slowly down the street like a float in a parade, but because of the size, the truck shifted from side to side, precariously making its way down the narrow road. As it pulled away, the gathered neighbors saw Yonathan had jumped onto the back of the truck and climbed up the steps leading to the front door of the house-in-tow.

"Get down from there!" Amare cried out as his son clung to the structure.

"Hold on tight, Yonathan," Gashe Ayeloo shouted from his open window as Marla screamed.

"He's going to fall! There's no space up there," Elsie yelled.

"Stop the truck," Tariq hollered, banging his hands on the driver-side door. The driver hit the brakes, and Yonathan jerked forward, then backward, clinging to the sill like a suction doll.

The driver looked over the crowd of exasperated neighbors as Tariq asked him to just wait, and the driver said, "Okay, take a little time, but," he added, "I need to get this truck back soon. It's a rental and I'm no Billionaire Gates."

"What are you doing?" Amare asked his son and climbed up next to him.

"How'd they do that?" Yonathan wondered, pointing at the window to the interior of the home.

"It looks like everything is all bolted down," said Amare. "Like a ship's furnishings maybe," he said.

"Is this a ship? Can a house be a ship?"

"I guess in a way some homes can," Amare replied.

"Why don't we take our home with us, too?" Yonathan asked.

Amare looked down the street to #374, its pristine facade, its trimmed hedges, the fresh paint, the windows so clean that he could see inside from where he stood.

"Not all homes can come with you," Amare said and turned to

find Yonathan wasn't standing beside him anymore but trying to walk around the side to see how the home was rigged.

"Someone help him," Amare yelled.

Tariq, already at the boy's side, tilted his always-lifted hands to Yonathan. "Hey there, be careful!" But Yonathan stepped back and away from Tariq, closer to the precarious mechanism of the rigging.

"I'm not coming down," Yonathan said. "I'm gonna bring my house up!"

Amare tried to pull him near, but there was so little space, and the house sloped down in the back, so it was hard for him to even manage his own weight. Gashe Ayeloo yelled from his open window, though not everyone could make out the words: "Get down! You never know what will happen to a home! Look out!"

"Dad, you gotta see this!" Yonathan said, and he made space for Amare at the ledge surrounding the floating house. "See, look inside. It's probably just as they left it," Yonathan marveled, and it seemed to be true. With this clearer view, they could see the rooms were filled with furniture, couches, tables, and chairs. The hutch and cabinets were still in the dining room, though stacked boxes lined the walls. There was a family photograph hanging in the main living room, and Amare looked up at the stairs like he expected a child to run down them to go play with the toys that were in the glass-faced cupboards.

At this point, the driver walked around to the back. He saw Amare standing tensely on the front steps, and Yonathan balancing on the narrow landing holding on to the banister. "Get down, you hoodlums," the driver yelled. "Trying to rob me before I've even arrived?" He started to lurch toward Yonathan, but Marla intervened.

"Baby, come down!" Marla said, crying out like the pain that hung in the air was her own. "Please, please, come over here."

"Hey Yonathan," Elsie shouted. "I've got something for you."

"What? A house like a ship?"

"No," Elsie said, but she held up the twenty-dollar bill that Hirwi had given her earlier that day. "A housewarming gift for your new place."

Yonathan considered the offer with wide eyes but pouted and snatched a cluster of shiny cottonwood fluff from the air, then picked at the soft white casing.

"Look, every home is different, Yonathan," Elsie said. "You might keep moving until you find the right one, but look inside. Is that your home? Does that feel like your home?"

"No," Yonathan said.

"Look at this family portrait," Elsie said, jumping up next to him. "Is that your family?"

"No," Yonathan said.

"And those toys are for children," Elsie added, pointing to the window. "Are you going to be a grown-up for us today?"

"Yes," Yonathan said like he was being asked if the earth orbited the sun.

Tariq walked close enough for Yonathan to lean into Tariq's lifted hands and carefully brought Yonathan down, the first time that any of his neighbors had seen Tariq lower his arms. Elsie approached Yonathan cuddled up in Tariq's embrace, then handed Yonathan the twenty. "I didn't come down for that," Yonathan said, refusing Elsie's money.

She nodded respectfully. "Then take it for a rainy day," she said, and at that, Yonathan accepted her gift.

"Time to start again, okay?" Aida said to him and gave him her phone card. "Call us, okay?"

"Okay, Miss Aida."

Tariq carried Yonathan to Mamush's cab, and Yonathan said

to Mamush, "My teacher told our class the world is mostly water, and I bet a house like a ship could cross an ocean, go with you anywhere."

Mamush replied, "Sometimes, like it or not, you have to put down new roots again, little guy, with or without a sense of peace." Yonathan's gaze followed the home that made its way to #374. The driver walked around the property searching for the right spot to anchor the house. Before he could pick the location, the 42 pulled up to the waiting passengers, who filed into the crowded bus, including Marla and Elsie.

"What a morning, huh?" Marla said, sitting down next to Elsie.

"It seems so," Elsie said and looked out the window as #374½ was being unhitched onto level land.

Marla continued, "Oh, what we all have been through to get here, what pains to leave our homes and start again, and we think that if we can just make it here, all will be well. Little do we realize that once we show up, that's when the hardest work begins, life's work. Leaving, crossing, arriving, pitching your home, that's prelude. The struggle, the letting go, that long voyage, that's all just prelude."

The bus turned off the cul-de-sac, and Marla and Elsie watched Mamush's cab pass them, Yonathan's hand sticking out the window catching the cottonwood seeds.

Marla scooted closer to Elsie and continued, "I could write a book on lessons for new immigrants. For your eyes and ears only, okay? First and foremost, trust no one who doesn't like the food you eat or the way you smell or the clothes you wear, and if you don't know if they like the food you eat or the way you smell or the look of you, better safe than sorry. Ultimately, you've got no real choice but to seek out a little help when you start over, but first and foremost, turn to those who like the food you eat and the clothes you wear and the scent of you. I've got a lot more free, priceless advice for new immigrants where that came from. Words to live by! You should know what I know," and Marla began imparting what wisdom came to mind, Elsie half-listening to the familiar words.

When the bus turned off MLK Ave., and after heading north a few more blocks, most of the passengers, a diverse group of travelers, disembarked, and a slew of new passengers, all white, got on. Marla dropped her voice, shifted her weight uncomfortably, and whispered, "Remind me to pick this all up again later. Marla's advice for new immigrants, for your ears and eyes only, to be continued—"

Swearing In,
January 20, 2009

I remember the cold first of all, the kind I embrace one day each winter when I check the cover on the tulip bulbs. I remember the Potomac stretched forth like a frozen arctic landing. And the wind glided over it, and it stung.

The tears in my eyes were as much for the ecstasy as for the cold.

I felt the great pride of having chosen my home wisely after all, my certainty tested when, for instance, I was told by my neighbors that my food smelled "too spoiled to eat" even though it was made for my housewarming with love and great effort by distant relatives. Or when I got "feedback" that my accent seemed too unprofessional for my brand new job. Or when the woman I worked with began to request my best assignments (she and my boss were old family friends, and I, always an outsider).

This moment mattered to someone like me who sacrificed personally believing in all this, these symbols, their message, the songs, the flag, the promise I trusted so profoundly that when it called out to me from thousands of miles away, I responded with everything I had. That faith rooted deep, and maybe this is why somehow, despite everything, an immigrant can be among the most patriotic of all a country's citizens.

Rows of jumbotrons stretched from the podium to the Washington Monument like billboards along a highway. The images from the stage reflected back again and again. I heard the words long after seeing them spoken on the telecast, a great slow echo passing over an expanse of red, white, and blue that I would have mistaken for a Fourth of July parade, except for the parkas and the Polartec.

I was there to witness with my own two eyes, and to hear with my own ears, the swearing in of this man whose father came from the part of the world I did, perhaps charmed by the same pledge.

Aretha sang "My Country 'Tis of Thee." Her voice rang like a meditative bell, her flight-and-dip gospel tone, the deep well of her melody reverberating over our millions. People around me were looking for signs everywhere. That Michelle wore a dress on a day like this was clear proof of her fortitude, someone noted. "That's the Lincoln Bible. The Lincoln Bible," a young woman with thick glasses and silver-blue streaks in her red hair shrieked. Then we all were still and silent as Roberts administered the oath. I paid careful attention to the words we were gathered there to hear. And we were silent and still as Stevens swore in Biden, and by then my toes were numb. But I stayed put to see the moment through.

The trek home was disorienting. Subways were a trap. Impossible, jammed up for miles. I walked back to Virginia amid spontaneity, sudden outbursts of song, of embracing. There was dancing in the streets.

I heard a man ask a boy I assumed was his son if the world looked different. The man held his son's wrists. The child wore his father's too-big gloves. Maybe it was inevitable that this man would remind me of my own father—dark skin, a neat afro picked up then patted down, that same rigid look of someone who'd quietly weathered life's tough experiences.

I thought of the distant country I'd left behind, the family who contributed what they could so I'd have enough for my journey (money, extra sweaters, pre-addressed and pre-stamped envelopes, parting words of advice). They thought everything would be different for me, and though the challenges were new, I faced obstacles here just as I struggled there, only this time under the heavy scrutiny of our collective hope.

I watched this child lift his gloved hands, jump up and down, and chant, "Hope! Change! Yes! We! Can!" The father leaned down and said to him, "You see this? You *feel* this? We'll bottle it up, take this back home with us. This will last us, this will last."

I wanted this to last, too, this feeling returned, this promise renewed, belief restored, everything feeling *possible* again. But what I didn't see then was that while a great hope sprung up in me on that January afternoon, a great fear arose in others. And ever since, I've witnessed that hope pitted against that fear, every stop as I traveled to Iowa to Brooklyn to Florida to Minnesota to Texas to L.A. before settling down in Seattle, foreshadowed or confirmed in the stories told to me by every friend I've met along the way. My hope persisted while that fear got louder and louder and louder. Loud like a siren when I was pulled over for going too slow and I raised my arms as high as they would go. Loud like an organized chant on the bus to "send them back" that forced me to find a place all the way in the last row of the downtown 42 and raise my arms again. Loud was that chorus that made me feel that I, that we, don't belong even though here we are. Loud was the chorus that made me keep my hands up in surrender and never put them down again, lift them ever to the sky just in case, and keep them up until I could receive what I'd come for—what we're all looking for—the peaceful promise of home, its safety, security, its embrace.

I think back to that January afternoon that was so steeped in hope that you could feel its warmth despite the numbing air. On the long walk back to my garden apartment where I would spend the rest of the day studying and carefully balancing spreadsheets of costs versus earnings versus what I could send to my family abroad, I knew then that the world must be the same as it had been the day before. Still, I wondered if I'd eventually look back to find something new and remarkable sprung up from that start, and if so, what that would turn out to be. And I walked along the banks of the icy river toward home over ground lit by that stark midwinter sun, thinking about the tulips.

Acknowledgments

It has been a profound experience preparing this debut book for publication over the course of this pandemic (these stories were submitted to the Restless Books Prize for New Immigrant Writing in Spring 2020, the prize was announced in Fall 2020, and we're preparing for publication in 2022). There has been something utterly moving knowing that even as I was editing during lockdowns and mega- then giga-fires here in the Bay Area, these pages were not meant for me alone. I imagine it would be meaningful no matter what to be working on the publication of a debut collection, but in the days when many of the shops on my street were closed to patrons and the roads were eerily empty, the writing process felt less like an act of expression and more like an important path to connection in these times. My first word of thanks go to the team at Restless Books and my editors, Nathan Rostron and Ilan Stavans for believing in these stories. It was an honor to have my writing recognized by the incredible guest judges for this year's prize as well: Dinaw Mengestu and Achy Obejas. Thank you to my agent, Julia Kardon, for her unwavering dedication and remarkable vision.

One of the pleasures of having a collection with so many published pieces is that it's given me the opportunity to connect with a range of wonderful editors and teams at such stellar publications that printed the earliest editions of these stories: *Ploughshares* ("The Drought That Drowned Us," 2020, guest editor Celeste Ng), Akashic Books' *Addis Ababa Noir*, ("Kind Stranger," 2020, editor Maaza Mengiste), *New England Review* (Medallion, 2020), *The Iowa Review* ("A Down Home Meal for These Difficult Times," 2018/2019), *Zyzzyva* ("The Street Sweep," 2018), *McSweeney's Quarterly Concern* ("The Wall," 2018, guest editor Nyuol Lueth Tong), *Indiana Review* ("Sinkholes," 2017), *The Offing* ("Preludes," 2016), *The Normal School* ("Swearing In, January 20, 2009," 2015), *Boulevard* ("Mekonnen aka Mack aka Huey Freakin' Newton," 2015), and *The Missouri Review* ("The Suitcase," 2015).

One of the challenges of having a collection that has come together over many years is properly thanking everyone who has made a difference to these pages, but I'm grateful for all of the generous encouragement that has sustained this work. A warm thank you to the Helen Zell Writers' program at the University of Michigan, my amazing teachers there with special thanks to Peter Ho Davies and Lorna Goodison, and my talented, brilliant, inspiring cohort. My appreciation to Yaddo, MacDowell, Ragdale, the Martha Heasley Cox Center for Steinbeck Studies at San Jose State University, Artist Trust, and the Elizabeth George Foundation for supporting my work. I'm grateful to the workshops, artists, writing groups, and creative thinkers I've learned from along the way, including my current Bay Area writing group (Ingrid, Yalitza, Angie, Amber, Melissa, Tanya, and Nancy). Most importantly, my sister Meklit, who has been essential to my work in too many ways to list here.

I'm honored that some of these stories have been recognized over time, particularly "The Suitcase" in *The Best American Short Stories* 2016, with "Mekonnen aka Mack aka Huey Freakin' Newton" and "Medallion" listed as notables in 2016 and 2021 respectively. I'd also like to thank *Selected Shorts* and Renée Elise Goldsberry of *Hamilton* for her stunning reading of "The Suitcase," which brought that story to life on the stage and on the radio. My deepest thanks to the AKO Caine Prize for African Writing for shortlisting my story "The Wall" in 2019 and choosing "The Street Sweep" as the 2021 winner. Thanks to the organizers of that award for lifting so many voices, to the writers recognized in both cohorts for their powerful work, and to everyone who has read and engaged with these stories over the years. And of course a final thank you to my family in the US and in Ethiopia—no matter how far away, always in my heart.

About the Author

MERON HADERO is an Ethiopian American who was born in Addis Ababa and came to the US via Germany as a young child. Meron's short stories have won the 2021 AKO Caine Prize for African Writing, have been shortlisted for the 2019 AKO Caine Prize for African Writing, and appear in *Best American Short Stories, Ploughshares, McSweeney's Quarterly Concern, Zyzzyva, The Iowa Review, Missouri Review, 40 Short Stories: A Portable Anthology*, and others. She's also been published in *The New York Times Book Review* and the anthology *The Displaced: Refugee Writers on Refugee Lives*, and will appear in the forthcoming anthology *Letter to a Stranger: Essays to the Ones Who Haunt Us*. A 2019–2020 Steinbeck Fellow at San Jose State University, and a fellow at Yaddo, Ragdale, and MacDowell, Meron holds an MFA in creative writing from the University of Michigan, a JD from Yale Law School (Washington State Bar), and a BA in history from Princeton with a certificate in American studies.

RESTLESS BOOKS is an independent, nonprofit publisher devoted to championing essential voices from around the world whose stories speak to us across linguistic and cultural borders. We seek extraordinary international literature for adults and young readers that feeds our restlessness: our hunger for new perspectives, passion for other cultures and languages, and eagerness to explore beyond the confines of the familiar.

Through cultural programming, we aim to celebrate immigrant writing and bring literature to underserved communities. We believe that immigrant stories are a vital component of our cultural consciousness; they help to ensure awareness of our communities, build empathy for our neighbors, and strengthen our democracy.

Visit us at restlessbooks.org